The Road to Somewhere

The Road to Somewhere

Helen Armstrong

Illustrated by Harry Horse

Orion
Children's Books

First published in 2001
by Orion Children's Books
a division of the Orion Publishing Group
Orion House
5 Upper St Martin's Lane
London WC2H 9EA

Text © Helen Armstrong 2001
Illustrations © Harry Horse 2001

The right of Helen Armstrong and Harry Horse to be
identified as the author and illustrator respectively
of this work has been asserted.

All rights reserved. No part of this publication may
be reproduced, stored in a retrieval system, or transmitted,
in any form or by any means, electronic, mechanical,
photocopying, recording or otherwise, without the
prior permission of Orion Children's Books.

A catalogue record of this book
is available from the British Library.

Typeset at The Spartan Press Ltd,
Lymington, Hants

Printed in Great Britain by
Clays Ltd, St Ives plc

ISBN 1 85881 845 1

*To Mrs Brenda Naylor and her class at
St Andrew's C of E Primary School at Skegby,
who heard this story first*

CHAPTER 1

Ratty. That's me.

I am round, brown, and nosy. Clever too. Just like you'd expect a ratty to be. I live here, on Farmer's farm, with my friends. This bright morning I am sitting in the barn, trying to find out why Cow is so sad.

Cow has been my friend since I was the smallest ratty you ever saw. And here she is, sad as sad can be.

'Oh Ratty,' says Cow, 'oh Ratty, it's the end for me. I've got a one way ticket now. Oh Ratty.'

My whiskers shake. What is she talking about? It sounds very bad.

'Oh Cow!' I say and my voice squeaks. 'What do you mean?'

'Cow' I call her but Number 129 is what it says on her humpy, lumpy, black and white back. I can't call her that! Number 129. It isn't friendly, you know. 'Hello 129!' 'Glad to see you 129!' You see what I mean? Can't be done.

So I call her Cow. That's pretty silly too you may say. There's lots of cows, so how do I know which one is my Cow? Well she is just different. She is my oldest special friend. I've known Cow since the day I first stepped out of the warm rat nest where my brothers were sleeping. Three steps from home and there she was, right here in this barn. She was as new as I was and as little as a cow can be, which is quite big.

We got on, we did, right from the start. Cow is a nice peaceful sort of person, though jumpy-lively for a cow. Me, I'm a bit of a fidget, but we get on. We get along a long while. And here she is, my friend, standing in the darkest corner of the barn, all sagging, ears flopping, eyes all dopey, sad as sad can be.

I jump up and perch on a hook that sticks out of the wall so that I can look into her long face. But she won't look at me. She looks down at her feet. Then she sighs so hard she almost blows me off my perch.

'Oh, Ratty,' she says. 'I'm a failure. Fail, no pass, no prizes, not up to it, bottom of the class. Oh ho, says Farmer, out you go and that is that.'

'What!' I say. 'What do you mean?' But there's a cold grip on my heart because I guess.

'Failed my standard. Useless thing. Not enough milk. It's out-you-go time. That is what Farmer says.'

'Out you go?' I say in a sort of whisper.

'Out I go,' she says. 'Me. The truck tomorrow. One, two, beef stew,' she says.

Not good, you must say. If it was a friend of yours? Not good.

'Certain definite?' I say.

'Certain definite sure,' she says. 'About time too! says Farmer. Waste of feed! he says. Off I go. To never-come-back.'

She is crying now. I look at her in silence. My friend. Going to never-come-back. No more friend. That's not good.

I try to think. Someone has to.

'What about...?' I say. 'What about you go somewhere else? Somewhere different?'

She lifts her head a bit and goggles at me. She has big sad eyes at the best of times but now they are like two big shiny tear-pools.

'Somewhere else?' she says.

These cows just don't get around, you know. It's a real problem in times like this. I don't suppose she's ever seen beyond the field hedge in her life. Her whole world is barn, milking parlour and one green field. Now we rats, citizens of the world we are. We see it all. I've even been to a town I tell you, and come back safe as your fluffy slippers. There and back, and no one the wiser. Except me of course.

'There's lots of places to go,' I say. 'You don't have to go to never-come-back. There's more than one way out of here,' I say, 'not just one road and one place to go. There's lots of roads. Lots of places.'

She's gawping now. Eyes popping, mouth open, boggled.

'Lots of places?' she says.

'Yes. Lots of places.' I'm thinking aloud now. 'What about not getting into that truck? What about going somewhere else instead? You could run, away from here!'

'Yes,' she says. She looks at me and her dark pooly eyes are glistening now, like water in a breeze. 'Now?' she says. 'Run now?'

'Oh, oh,' I say. 'Why now?'

'Why not?' she says. Sometimes these cows surprise you, they do.

'Why not?' I say. 'Yes indeed. But wait,' I say, 'wait a moment.'

I have no plan, no plan at all. I need just a microsecond, for thinking. So I think for just a breath. Then I take a quick look out of the barn door.

'Not now,' I say. 'Doggo in the yard. Farmer at the house door. Tractor in the lane. Later. I'll watch out. I'll tell you. Be ready.'

'Ready, ready,' she says, 'ever-ready, quick to start, quick to go. Ready!' and she skips about where she stands.

I can see why she's useless at this milking thing. Cows that do the business in the milk way are the calm ones, the great big solid ones, with nothing in their heads but breathing and eating and turning it all into more of the white stuff.

Here she is, skipping like a pony, all dancing and quick, shaking her patterned head and whisking her tail. Not the temperament, I think. Not suited. Needs another job entirely. More for me to think about.

And that's what I'm doing two hours later,

thinking away, sitting by a wall, stroking my oh so long whiskers when...

'Now!' – breathes a soft excited sort of voice somewhere over my head and there she is. Cow. Out and about. Dancing on her forked feet and ready for the off. 'Run now!' says she. 'All clear now!'

I bury my nose in my paws for just that microsecond but no more thinking comes. So I hop, skip, up her big nose as she leans it down for me. I scrabble over her curly forehead and grab hold of one warm pink-lined ear.

'Tickles!' she squeals and shakes her head giggling but then she straightens up and sets off in her own sweet time.

Step, step, she goes. Sway, sway, shimmer. I've not been on a cow before. As she walks her whole body has a sort of wiggle, a sway. It's when she moves her back leg up on each side. So, up here on her head I see the world move from one side to the other, sway, sway, shake. Bits of the road appear and then rush off sideways and then back again.

I love it. Rats see a lot, yes, but all low down. Perhaps Cow is not the dumb-dumb I have thought her. Perhaps she sees more than I do. Certainly she sees the white thing first.

Right in front of us. A round white curly thing standing on its four legs and blocking the gateway.

'Stop,' says the white thing. 'I's coming too.'

'Cat and Red Teeth!' I think. 'What next?'

For it is Woolly Woolly Baa Lamb, fierce and white and stamping his hard little hoof.

'I's coming too,' says Woolly Woolly Baa Lamb.

'Hello,' says Cow, friendly as ever. 'Happy to see you. We're off. Don't know where. To Somewhere. Somewhere else!'

'Somewhere?' says Woolly, breathing out through his tight white nose. 'Somewhere sounds good to me.'

He points his white nose to his round white rump. 'I's got a number,' he says. 'Numbers is bad news.'

There it is. Number 564 clear as paint upon his curly back.

Numbers are bad news. He's right there. I stroke my unnumbered shining fur with a warm paw.

'Names is best,' he says. 'Lambs with numbers is no news at all.'

It is true. There are lots of lambs in the spring. Some get names – Flora, Flossie, Bettybaa, Freda. They stay, those ones with names stay. I see them the next year and the next.

But most lambs get numbers. And lambs with numbers go away and never-come-back. Woolly Woolly Baa Lamb is right. He's on the ball, he's got the answer. Numbers are no news at all.

He hasn't waited for us of course. He falls in beside Cow, blinking his fierce little eye and jabbing at the road with his hard little hoofs.

Cow leans down her big head to sniff his nose. Then he sees me.

'Ratty!' he cries, jumping in the air. 'Ratty! Why is Ratty here? Ratty's no good, says my ma. What's he doing here?'

I feel crushed I can tell you. I haven't said anything but perhaps you knew. Rats are not everyone's favourites, no we are not. People don't like us. Farmer doesn't. And lots of the animals don't like us either.

Cows aren't much bothered by us rats, so Cow's mother never told her that I wasn't the kind of friend a cow would want to be seen with. And now this.

'Ratty is nice,' says Cow. 'Ratty's a finker-head, clever-finker head. Pretty too,' she says, 'kind. My friend.'

Well I lay my head down upon my paws and I weep. Never, not in all life, has anyone said so much.

'Oh Cow,' I say into her pink-lined velvet ear. 'Oh

Cow.' My tears trickle into the pink folds so that she laughs and shakes her head.

'Tickles!' she squeaks and does another little dance.

I am silent. I have nothing to say. But Woolly Woolly Baa Lamb always has his word.

'Well,' says he, 'I may be wrong. Could be. Clever finker thinker is he?' He isn't sure I can tell. 'Need to be off though, and any friend is a good friend on a clear road which is now.'

He is right again, for the long farm track is clear. Nothing stirs as far as the eye can see.

'Come,' says Cow. So the two of them trot along side by side, all out of step and me lurching about on Cow's head trying to keep my breakfast down. This swing, swing, shimmer is a bit rough when Cow is trotting I can tell you.

We get to the lane end and look about us. The road is here, clear as can be. It is hard under hoof, and goes each way. But which way for us?

Just then, as we stand and look and shake our three heads, just then, with a growl and a snarl, comes Doggo. He is round us like a flash and standing between us and the road, Wall-Eyed Doggo, the Farmer's Friend.

CHAPTER 2

Here we are, right at the road now, almost escaped, and here is Doggo, straight in front of us and blocking the way. He shows his teeth. He looks very fierce indeed.

What is to happen next I wonder?

'What's up?' says Doggo. 'What's up and where are you off to?'

'Oh Doggo,' says Cow looking at him in her trusting sort of way. 'Off I go tomorrow you see, and Baa Lamb's got a number too. Both off to never-come-back. Ratty says – go somewhere else! Good finker Ratty!'

Doggo looks at her. For a long time. We wait.

What else?

'My job,' says Doggo, 'is to look after you, Number One. My job is to keep you safe,' says he, 'Number Two. You're travelling, not staying,' says he, 'so, Number Three, I help you to travel. Trust me!' says Wall-Eyed Doggo.

I am speechless. This is Doggo talking, the Farmer's Friend. He has managed to scramble his head into helping us – or that's how it sounds. He's called Wall-Eyed by the way because he has two pale mottled eyes which make him look blind. But he is not. As any sheep can tell you. And he is Farmer's Friend.

But not now. Why?

Doggo sees me on Cow's head. He sees me thinking too.

'There's a new dog on the block,' he says to me, nodding his head to the question I haven't asked. 'Farmer's gone and bought a new dog. After all this time! A puppy! Never asked me, did he? Well Farmer can lump it!' So says Wall-Eyed Doggo.

I understand. I have seen the new pup. He's already bigger than Doggo. Farmer thinks he's the sun in the sky. He shows him off to all his farmer friends. 'Prize-winning stock,' says Farmer, 'star in the making.' All the while Wall-Eyed Doggo sits in a grey lump in the corner of the yard, half closing his pale eyes.

Well, yes, I think. Perhaps. But I look hard at Doggo. I wish I was certain. I look at Doggo as hard as hard can be. He looks back. He smiles at me in his doggo way and blinks his grey and marbled eyes. I hope that we can trust him.

All three of us nod our heads, very slow. 'We trust you,' we say.

I have my little paws crossed I can tell you and Woolly is standing a bit lopsided too. But what choice do we have?

'Well,' says Doggo, 'you won't get far on a road. Someone will see you and call Farmer. They will report you as a risk to life and limb. You need to find another way. You need me to show you.

'This way,' says Doggo. He nods his grey head along the road to where it disappears into a hollow between trees.

'This way and keep in tight,' he says, bossy as ever. We trot along that road, Cow in front (plus me of course) and Woolly Woolly Baa Lamb, then Doggo at the back. In a row, tight to the edge of the road, doing what he tells us, which is what Doggos like, as you will find.

Then a car engine – I hear it straight ahead and

coming towards us. I see it from my high perch. Here's the car, coming towards us and slowing down.

'Oh no,' I say to myself. 'Oh no, ruin already. Somewhere is nowhere after all.'

But no. The car slows down. Two little girls peer out at us.

'Look! Look! Mum, Dad!' they cry. Everyone is smiling inside the car. They wave and point to Doggo. Then they are past and moving on.

Doggo looks twice as big and twice as bossy as before.

'You see,' says he, 'you're all right with me here. They think I am a trusted Farmer's Friend doing my job,' he says. 'They can see I am a responsible animal.'

'Well,' I say sort of softly to myself, 'I don't know what Farmer would think about that if he could see you now.'

It is soft but he hears it because doggos have clever ears that I will say. He falls silent for a while and gets a sort of crease on his furry forehead.

'Anyway,' I say more loudly now, 'we are going to do this on our own so where is this place you're showing us? I hope it's good.'

'Patience, patience,' says Wall-Eyed Doggo. 'Soon enough, just here in fact.'

Doggo stops. Cow and Woolly Woolly Baa Lamb

step onto the green verge of the road. We see, through gates on both sides of the road, a straight line of path. It stretches into the distance, as far as the eye can see. A track, a hard raised track, overgrown with shrubs and trees on each side. It is like a long green tunnel.

'This is it,' he says, 'the railway.'

'The rail way?' I say to him. 'What rail way? What rails? I see no rails.'

'Used to be,' says he. 'Used to be trains here. Blue and white they were, rattling along, people inside looking out. All glass at the side. Go faster than a doggo can run. With big wheels. Big squashing wheels.'

'But not now?' I say. I don't like all this talk of squashing wheels. My Uncle Alfred went under a squashing wheel so the story goes and I liked Uncle Alfred.

'No, not here now,' says Doggo. 'It's a path now. Path to where? I don't know.' He stops and looks around him. He has no more to say.

'OK,' I say into Cow's ear. She is a bit tired after her trot along the road. She is reaching to curl her long tongue around a clump of green young grass by the path edge. 'OK,' I say. 'This is it.' Woolly Baa Lamb is taking a quick bite at some green grass too.

'Herbivores,' says Wall-Eyed Doggo, in a bored sort of voice. 'Eating is what they do best.' He looks at me perched on Cow's head. 'As you will find.'

'You snob!' says Woolly Woolly Baa Lamb. 'When did I see you turn your nose up at food, Doggo, greedy Doggo, my friend?'

Woolly is a tough character I will say, sheep or no. Doggo's teeth don't impress him though perhaps they should. Doggo looks at him thoughtfully but says nothing, then turns on his shaggy paws.

'Bye folks,' he says. 'Good luck. Good eating. Good sleeping and a safe journey's end.'

That's handsome I think. That's kind.

We nod our heads at him. He has been our friend when we needed him and we are grateful. He trots off waving his plumey tail. Then suddenly he stops and pauses and turns back.

'One thing,' he says. 'Doggos. Any doggo with a sparkle in his eye will chase you, bound to. One thing to try – should work – with most doggos. Just say – *friends under the fur.*'

'What does it mean?' I say to him. Doggos are funny things but this sounds silly even for a doggo.

Doggo blinks a little. He looks embarrassed. 'It's from a doggo rhyme,' says he. 'Goes like this –

> *Hoof or paw,*
> *Tame or free,*
> *Under the fur,*
> *Friends are we.*

'Haven't heard it for a while,' says he, 'but I think that's how it goes. Don't need to say it all though. Just say *friends under the fur*. Should be enough. Should stop doggos. Most doggos. I think.' He looks a bit thoughtful and so am I.

'You think!' I squeak. 'There's confidence for you.' But he is trying to help and it is all we have. 'Thank you Doggo, many thanks, and good luck yourself my friend.'

'Good luck,' we all cry. This time he trots off down the road and doesn't turn round.

'All on our own,' says Woolly Woolly Baa Lamb.

'All on our own,' I say. My whiskers are trembling. My heart is jumping in my chest. Cow is breathing hard.

Woolly looks a touch whiter than usual. 'New thing for me,' he explains. 'Sheep go with sheep, you understand. All stick together and never stand out, that's what my mother told me.'

'Yes,' I reply. 'And that's why you came with us. All stick together and into the van you go. To never-come-back. That's the truth.'

'That's the truth too,' he says, 'that is the truth.'

Cow is looking up and down the path, quietly, carefully. She points her long nose forward. 'This way?' she says to no one in particular.

Why not?

So I make myself comfortable on her high head.

Woolly Woolly Baa Lamb takes a last bite of the green grass by the path. We set off at a trot along the leafy tunnel of the path.

That track is straight as a farmer's stick. From my high seat I can see a long way ahead and even, if Cow turns her ears a little, a long way back behind us.

'Keep a watch out,' says Woolly.

'What do you think I'm doing?' says I. 'My eyes are popping with watching out!'

I am cross. They have had a bite of grass but I've missed out. Now my stomach is like a hole in the ground.

I blink with crossness. I almost miss it.

'Oh dear,' I cry out, 'oh dear.' A speck, a jumping running speck in the distance. A doggo. A long way off but coming closer.

'Oh friends,' I cry, 'a doggo. With teeth no doubt. And with a Person Friend too I am sure.'

'Hide!' says Cow.

Now there's a poser.

I can hide, easy beasy, quick as thinking. Perhaps Woolly can hide too. He can, he does, quick as a white fluffy flash. Down the bank he goes, through the wire fence and into the green field beyond. Hey presto, there he is, a sheep in a green field, eating the grass, nothing to notice, safe as can be.

He puts his head down and munches.

'I'm a sheep,' he says, 'minding my own business.

It's a bad dog that chases me. I'm safe.' He waggles his tail and looks pleased with himself. 'Safe. This grass is good I must say.'

'You're safe, yes!' I call out, 'but what about Cow?'

'Oh!' says Woolly Woolly Baa Lamb. His white face is suddenly long and sad and sorry. 'Oh dear friends, I had forgotten. We are together and Cow is so big. Oh Cow!' he says, almost crying as he looks at her.

But Cow has her own ideas. She snorts. Then she turns and skids down off the path with her big forked feet. She crashes down the bank under the tangled shrubs. There is a wet dark ditch under the branches. Into it she goes. Then she lies down in the black ditch mud, under the sheltering leaves.

Not easy. Have you seen a cow lie down? They take all day about it – not like you and me, a little bend of the legs and down we go. No – they stretch their heads out, bend their knees, kneel, look about them, and then flop their back legs down with a sort of gaspy groan. Hard work.

Still down she goes and down she is at last.

She lays her long dappled neck in the mud and lies as still as a rock, while the leaves above her head blow in the breeze.

As for me, with a hop and a leap, I'm up a tree.

Just in time. Here comes Stranger Doggo, sniffing

about and thinking of nothing in particular. We can see his Friend behind him, no Farmer this time, but a Lady in a big hat who waves a stick and hums as she walks.

'Tum tee tum,' she says, 'tum tee tum.'

Stranger Doggo is sniffing along the path, waving his short tail and looking about him as he goes. He has seen Woolly Woolly Baa Lamb in the field. He thinks about giving him a little run for his money, but he looks back at his Friend who is close behind. He decides to give it a miss this time. Then, he reaches the place where Cow left the path.

He jams his paws into the mud. He puts his sniffing sniffing nose to the ground. He breathes in cow smell until his head must spin. 'Cow,' he says, yapping loud and high. 'Cow. I smell Cow. Here's Cow!'

He looks about him in a wild sort of way.

'What have you got there, Bono?' says his Friend who is coming up fast. Doggo does not reply because he cannot believe his nose. He sees no cow but cow there is. That is what his nose tells him.

He sticks his nose to where Cow took her slide. He sniffs again. Then he begins to come towards us, down through the grasses and the tangled shrubs. 'Cow,' he mutters to himself as he comes. 'Cow. I know it. Cow is here somewhere.'

Then he looks up. He sees me on my branch.

'Oh Ratty,' he says with a nasty leer upon his face. 'Cow or not, you are fair game, my friend, that I know. Come down from that branch, my furry fleeing friend and let me chop you up.'

'I think not,' I say.

Even as I speak he sees Cow or a bit of Cow down below him in the mud. He stops again. Every hair on his back is stiff with astonishment.

'I knew it,' he yaps. 'Cow and Ratty too. Oh my day, it is my day. Games. Chasing. Oh good times now.' He grins a wolfy toothy grin that I don't like at all.

Now is the time to try it. *'Under the fur,'* I whisper in a high hissy voice so that the Lady in the big hat doesn't hear me. *'Friends under the fur.'*

He stops his sniffing. He stops his step forward in mid-stretch. His tail droops.

'Oh,' he says. 'Oh dear, oh dear.' His ears move down a notch. He lets all the breath out of his body in a loud wuff.

'Oh dear,' says he. 'That's it then. Friends then. No chasing, no good time? But friends. Really?'

He is still hopeful I see. 'All of you?' he asks, licking his lips, just a quick flick. 'That's Cow too?' He looks at me sharpish.

'All of us,' I say. 'All. And that's the lambkin as well I had better say, before you think again of that.'

'Not my day. Not my time,' says Bono. 'Happy to

meet you of course. Very happy, I'm sure.' He doesn't sound as sure as he could be. 'Be safe,' he calls back over his shoulder as he turns.

'Whoops, just in time...' He scrabbles back up the bank, waving his tail in a foolish sort of way. He yaps to his Friend who is slowing down to see where he has gone.

'Oh there you are,' says she. Bono jumps in front of her and scurries away, leading her off. 'Rabbits I suppose,' she says to herself. On she goes, clump clumping her feet and tum tee tumming as she disappears into the green tunnel.

'Thanks friend,' I call after. He pauses and turns his head. He winks into the shadows which hide us. He wags his short and tufty tail to say he has heard me. He gives a little bound and disappears with a last flash of white and brown.

We listen as the clump clumping and the tum tee tum fade into the distance.

'Oh that was too scary,' says Woolly Woolly Baa Lamb. 'I need something to eat. I need a snack. I need a quiet field and a lie down.'

'Me too,' says Cow. 'Not safe in daytime is it Ratty? Not safe. Not all doggos are good friends perhaps?'

'Right,' I say for I am shaken up too. 'Right and right again. It's not safe now but night-time we will get along fine. It's a grand path and smooth and straight and we can get to Somewhere just as well in the dark as we can in the light.'

'Good finking Ratty,' says Cow. 'Grass Time now. Chew Time. Lie Down Time.'

I have to tell you that Chew Time for cows, Grass Time for cows is more than you would bargain for. They eat and eat but that's just Part One. Part Two is when they lie down and pull it all back into their mouths, bit by bit, and chew, chew, chew it all again. Then they swallow and down it goes good and proper. What a system I say. How long would ratties last if they took that long to get their food down them? Not long I can tell you, but, like Doggo says, herbivores are the way they are and that's all there is to it. So patience Ratty, I say to myself.

Cow needs a quiet field to eat and chew and lie down in. Or else she will be going nowhere next day nor me neither. Woolly Woolly Baa Lamb is happy as can be at this very minute because he's up to his knees in green grass. His tight little mouth is opening and shutting like a combine harvester.

'Cow,' says Woolly through a mouthful of grass, 'there is an open gate along there so why don't you come in here and make yourself comfortable.'

He sinks his head into the green again. All I can see are the twitching tops of his white ears.

'Good finking Woolly,' says Cow. She stands up on her feet and shakes the wet ditch mud off her

back. Then she carefully clambers back onto the path and ambles the short way to the open gate.

'Grass Time,' she says with a long happy sigh. She steps into the sweeping grass with her mouth going munch munch munch.

'OK,' I say, 'food time for me too.' So down I hop and slide and scurry off, to find berries and mushrooms and seeds. I eat until my glossy belly is round and smooth. Then I climb slowly back up Cow's shoulder. She is lying down now – she is at the chewing stage. I curl up in her pink-lined ear and fall into a dozy sleep while her moving jaws grind away below my head, clunk, clunk, clunk.

The sky begins to darken. I can even see a star or two through my half-shut eyes. Suddenly, up I sit. What is that? I turn my big round ears to catch a sound. A sniffing, snuffing sound. There it is again!

Somewhere in the dark of the track is a hunting sniffing creature. Who can it be?

I listen, and listen, but the sound has stopped. There is no movement that I can see along the track.

I am tired. My eyelids close. I sleep once more. I sleep until the light has faded good and proper. When I open my eyes the dark has settled down on us and all I can see of Woolly is a pale blob lying in the long grass.

CHAPTER 3

'Is it time to go?' says Cow, swallowing her last mouthful (second time around that is of course).

'Yes, yes,' I say into her ear. I am wide awake now and I am worried. We are still too close to Farmer. I remember the sniffing shadow. 'Yes yes we must go and soon!'

A white owl comes skimming low over the long grasses.

'Screeech!' he goes as he sweeps past the three of us. 'Screeech!' He flaps his silent wings and soars off to find his supper.

The owl wakes Woolly. 'Where are we going now?' he says, crossly. 'Somewhere is what you said. Well, this is somewhere isn't it?'

'Not safe here,' says Cow. How right she is. 'Somewhere safe. That's what I want. Not safe here,' says Cow. 'Move-on-time I think Ratty.'

'Yes,' I say. 'Move-on-time. And double quick too.'

Woolly stands up and shakes his round body.

'Which way?' he asks.

'Same as before,' I say, 'that way down the straight track.'

So Cow gets up all lurching and swaying. The evening breeze is cool now. Up on Cow's head, high above the ground, the wind hits hard. Woolly has one last stretch and we set off, out of the gate, up the bank and along the dark tunnel of trees.

It is black dark now but easy enough for us to trot along. A smooth track. No turns. No bends. These trains were clever finkers I say to myself. Then I laugh so much that Cow asks me if I'm all right. 'Fine,' I say, and giggle on. A straight track to Somewhere. Good-luck-time I think.

We hear the whispering gossip of rabbits on either side as we trot on, but they don't mind us. Moths fly about us. An old fox sidles past.

'Evening folks,' he says and goes on his way. No questions from him, only rabbit thoughts in his head. The whispers fall silent until his foxy feet have trotted away out of hearing into the gloom.

We do well. A long way we go, always straight ahead, sometimes talking, sometimes silent. It is the blackest dark time of night when we stop at last for a quiet breath.

'Ratty,' says Cow, 'is that the sun?'

I look ahead and see a light. Not the sun, no, but what? Not on the track but to one side, glistening through the tree trunks and the scrubby bushes.

'Not the sun,' I say. 'But I don't know what it is. Don't know at all.'

It has me a bit worried, that light. I've seen the sheep trucks and the cattle trucks drive into Farmer's yard late in the evening. I've seen the way their long bright lights search out the dark corners, me in one of them as like as not. This looks too like that for my comfort, or Cow's, or Woolly's.

Then the light quenches suddenly into two dim glows. That doesn't cheer me at all. That's what you'd expect if a truck had stopped to wait for something. For what? And why here?

'Watch out,' I say. 'Quiet. Careful. Slow. Let's see what's what.'

So Cow steps forward as if her flat forked feet were soft slippers. Woolly sets his little sharp feet to the ground as if he was a spider creeping up to a fly. I cling on tight and peer forward to see what I can see.

'Oh oh,' says Cow blowing through her big nostrils, 'oh, oh,' she says, quiet as can be but frightened sounding. 'Big van. A big truck. Cow truck perhaps.' She almost wails if you can wail in a very very quiet sort of way.

It is a big truck, and it is parked right below us. We see now there is a dark road below us here, a curved road. On the corner of the road is a house, a big, high house, with wide iron gates and dark windows. In front of the house is a big van. Its back door is wide open. Between the house and the truck run two men, back and forwards, back and forwards, carrying things. The house lights are not on but they have their own lights and see what they want. They are wearing torches on their heads.

'They are feeding the van,' says Woolly. He is right. The men are feeding it chairs, and sofas, and boxes and pictures. They scurry into the house, out of sight for a moment, and then back, and into the van goes the next thing.

'Not good,' says Cow. 'Not good.'

'Bad men,' says Woolly. 'It's a takeaway truck. All those things are going to never-come-back.'

Right, I think, right. And only us to see.

'Bad truck,' says Woolly, 'greedy truck. Eat us all up too, quick as blinking, it would, if it knew we were here.'

'Stop them,' says Cow. 'We can.'

'Yes,' bleats Woolly in a fierce hiss, 'yes yes. We'll stop them. Save the chairs! Save the boxes! Stop the greedy truck!' He wags his tail and shakes his head as if he has horns which he does not.

'How?' I say. I whisper though I don't think the men are noticing much. It's all trot, trot, pick up, trot, trot, with them.

'Spooking,' says Cow, her eyes all twinkling bright, 'spooking.'

'Oh me too, me too,' says Woolly, dancing on his sharp little feet. 'Oh yes me too. Frighten the bad men! Stop the greedy truck! Oh yes oh yes!'

Well there you go. Herbivores for you. All surprises. All action when you don't expect it.

'Yes,' I say, 'yes, yes let's do it!'

First Woolly makes his careful way down through the tangle of shrubs. He checks out each step. 'It's all right here Cow,' he says, 'this way now,' he says.

Cow follows step by step. Me too of course, up on her head, riding high through the branches till here we are, right by the dark road. Straight opposite is the gate to the house. The big truck with its not-so-bright lights is right in front of us.

'I'll go this way,' says Woolly in a sort of hissing bleat. Off he goes into the dark as quiet as can be.

'Me this way,' says Cow. She nods her head the other way – gives me an anxious moment I can tell you. I have to hang on tight with all four paws and no mistake.

'Sorry Ratty,' says Cow. Then quiet as quiet she walks along the road, soft as her flat broad feet will take her, by the garden hedge, until she is looking over a side gate. There in front of us we see the open front door of the house, and the men, trotting and lifting, feeding the truck and not minding anything else.

Whoosh! Above our heads. White Owl is back again, wanting to know what's going on.

'Scuse me,' he says and lands like a feather on the gate beside Cow's head. 'Scuse me,' he says. 'You planning fun perhaps?'

'Yes,' says Cow, 'we'll stop them we will.'

'May I help?' says Owl. 'Frightening is my thing you know. Furry voles mainly. I'd like to scare people for a change,' he says hopefully.

'All help welcome,' says I. Owl squints a bit when he hears my voice. I know better than to move when Owl is around. He hasn't seen me until now. When he does, he narrows his eyes. I see he thinks that I look tastier than a vole. He wishes I wasn't so safe and tight between Cow's curved horns. But he is philosophical as owls are and takes it well.

'Can you get us started?' I ask.

'Happy to,' says White Owl. He rises silent smooth into the air. He hangs for a moment on his white wings. Then he swoops, low and sudden, over the men's heads as they trot out of the house.

'Screeeeeeeeeech!' he goes and flaps his white wings in their faces. 'Screeeeeeech!'

'Aaaaaaaaaaaaaah,' they both cry. They drop the table they are carrying and put their arms around their heads. 'Aaaaaaaaaah.'

'Baaaaa baaaaaa baaaaaa,' howls Woolly Woolly Baa Lamb from the shadows beyond. He hurls his white shape at their legs. Down they go, feet in the air, squealing.

'Ghosts! Ghosts!' says the little one. 'It's haunted, Jake. I knew it! I knew it!'

'Can't be, can't be,' says tall Jake, but his hands are over his face and he is peeping through his fingers. He is not sure about it at all, I can see.

Then Cow begins. I feel her take her breath into her long lungs. The air sucks in under my feet, her sides broaden, her back ripples and then – the noise begins.

What a noise. Not a moo at all. Not a cow noise you've ever heard but a long wailing howling sort of noise. It pours out of her mouth and fills the dark garden.

'OOOoooooooooooooow,' goes Cow.

'Eeeeeeeeeeeeh,' go the men. They leap up and into the cabin of the truck. They turn on the engine and try to get out of the gate. Backwards, forwards, backwards, forwards they go, until at last they get it right. They roar out of the gate, two wheels at

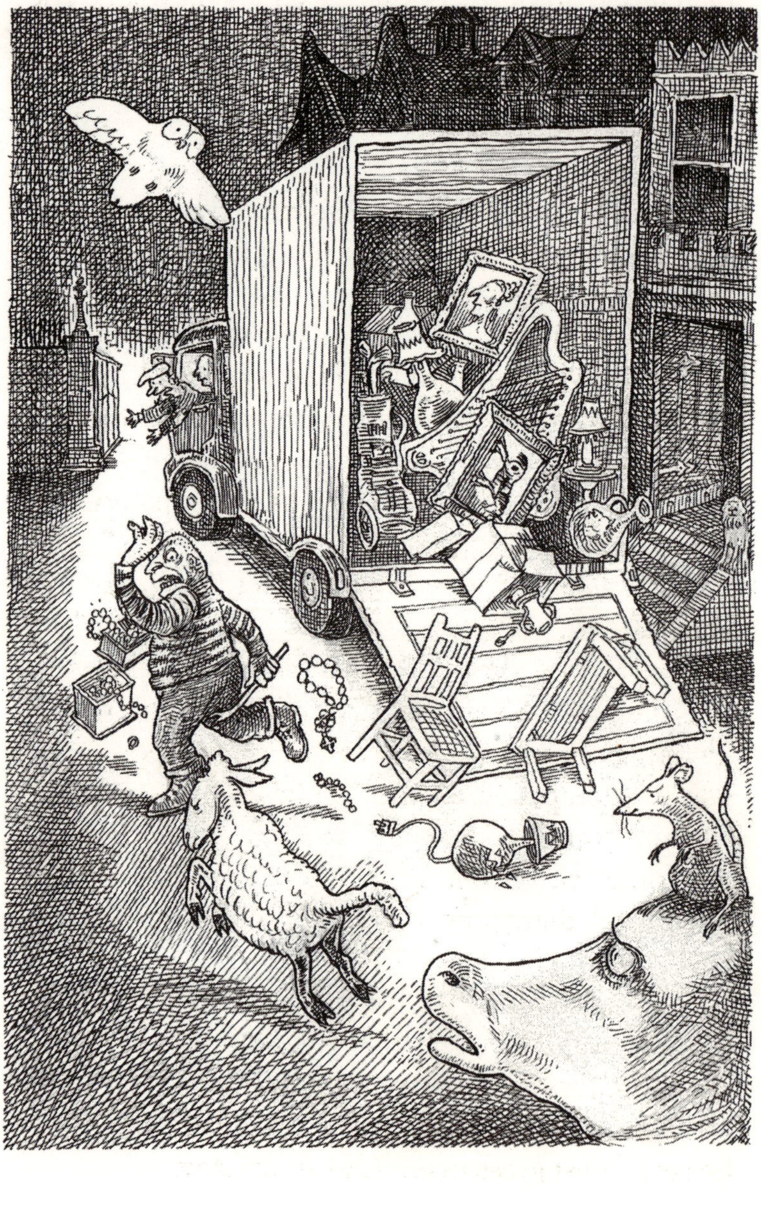

the corner, and off they go as fast as they can. The back door is still open. They spill furniture as they go.

'Your fault!' 'No it's not!' 'I told you! Ghosts! Vampires they were!'

We hear them into the distance, shouting and arguing over the engine roar, until the night covers them and silence returns.

'I liked that,' says Cow. 'Fun.' She blinks happily.

'Oh Cow,' says Woolly, 'that was good.' He is happy as can be. 'I chased them. I chased them! I like it. Can I chase somebody else soon?' I look down at Cow. She looks up at me. Perhaps not, we think, this could get out of hand.

Owl sweeps down over us and flaps his soft wings.

'Nice work,' says Owl. 'Don't know your names but nice work. Neat trick. Glad to meet you but I've got mice to catch. Got to go. Bye.' Off he goes with a few silent flaps into the dark sky.

'Well,' I say, 'Cow and Woolly, we've earned a rest, don't you think. What about here? It's almost dawn and there's no one about. No other houses either as far as I can see.'

'Yes,' says Woolly, 'that suits me. It's black as your big ears here, Cow, but this under my feet is grass, I can tell. Grass as sweet as new hay. A treat.' He curls his short upper lip and nibbles blissfully. 'Lovely,' he says. 'Best grass ever.' And so we stay.

CHAPTER 4

Next morning the sun rises in the sky, the birds wake up and we are all three as comfortable as can be.

Cow is lying in a big black and white heap on the lawn, chewing and chewing, with her eyes closed. Woolly Woolly Baa Lamb has fallen asleep in the shade of the hedge, his little feet stuck out sideways, looking as dead as mutton (if you'll excuse me mentioning it), except for his sides which go up and down, up and down as he breathes. And me? Well, I've had a scuttle round the dustbins. I've found some very nice things indeed, thank you, very tasty, very smelly. Just my style. So now I'm lying, paws in the air, eyes closed, in the hot sun on the porch. It is all as nice as nice can be.

When...roar, crunch, round the corner spins a big red car and flump! it pulls to a halt right in front of us.

I scream. I do. Just the shock of it, but it doesn't matter because someone else is screaming, too. It is a tall lady who is sitting in the front of the car, her mouth wide open, her eyes round like saucers and her hair standing on end.

'AAAAH!' she screams. 'AAAAAAh. There is a cow on the lawn!'

'Aah!' squawks the man beside her, not quite so loud. He is little and fat. He has a shiny bald head. 'Aah! My dear, there is a sheep in the hedge!' Because by this time even Woolly has woken up. He is half sitting, half standing under the hedge, blinking his fierce little eyes, and yawning with his tight white little mouth.

'AAAH most of all AAAh!' shouts the lady. She is a real screamer this one, for sure. 'There is a rat on the porch!'

She steps out of the car and puts her dainty shoe into a large cowpat that Cow produced an hour or so ago. She doesn't notice that. She is staring at me. 'A rat!' she squeals.

I wonder if she is going to faint but she does not. She stands there, eyes popping, and gawping at me as hard as she can go.

I am just about calm again. As long as there is no dog I am safe. I can outrun a tall lady and a fat man any day of the week.

And then, from the car, long, smooth, elegant as

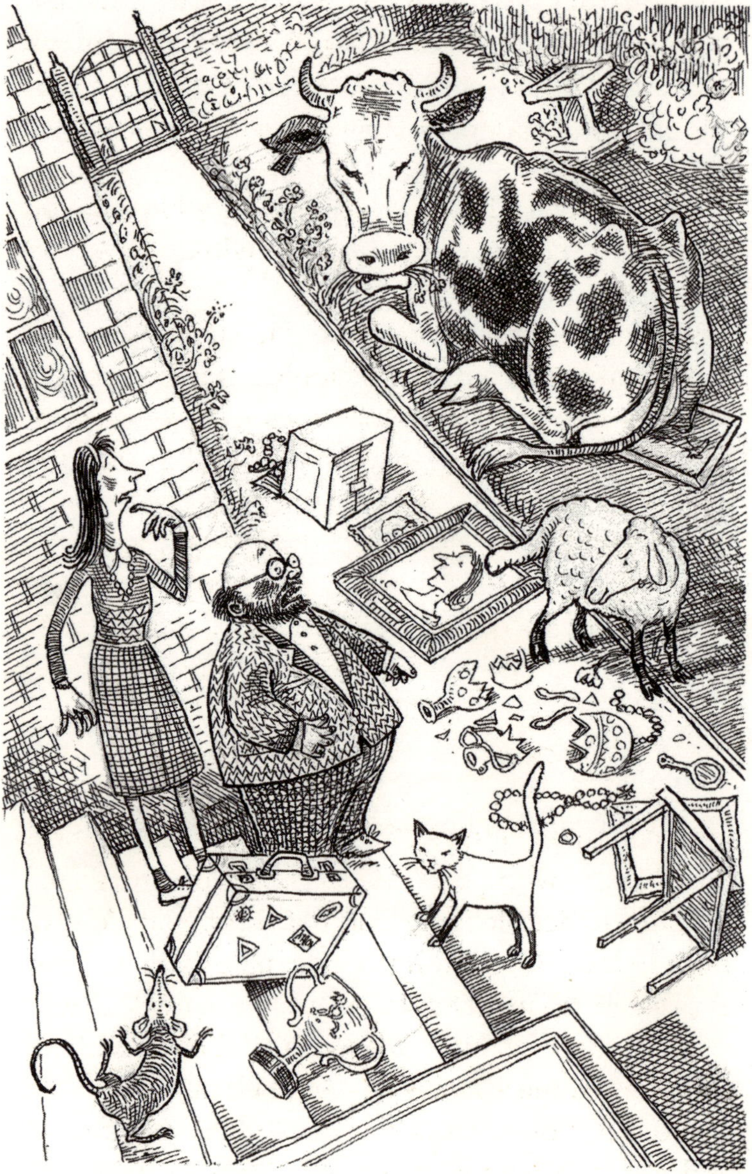

coffee cream, comes a cat. He is a big cat, and muscly under that smooth and velvet fur. Brown paws, brown ears and the bluest eyes you ever did see. Eyes like crystal pools and he has them fixed on me.

'Oh whoops,' I say to myself. 'Trouble for you Ratty I do believe. Get your little twinkly paws out of this one, my dear!'

But the cat makes no move. He stands there by the car like a cream and breathing statue. Then he looks round. He's a cat that likes to take his time. Cool he may be but even his cool crystal eyes widen a little as he sees Cow and Woolly. They widen more when he sees the table dropped upon its side on the lawn, and the coffee pot in the hedge where it bounced off the back of the van. Then worst of all – his eyes flash at this – he sees the front door open behind me.

He stretches out a soft paw. He pats the Tall Lady's leg.

'Excuse me,' he says in a voice like warm oil, best and thickest warm oil. 'Look around you, my dear.'

The lady does look around her. She begins to take it all in. Her face crumples, her mouth closes, her eyes screw up into sad little slits. She starts to cry.

'We've been robbed,' she wails. 'Robbed. Robbed. Oh, darling, the animals have robbed us.'

'Now my dear,' says the man, short and round and roly poly, climbing out of his side of the car. 'I don't think so. I'm sure Cinnamon here will tell us but I think not, you know. This is people's work. I can see boot marks here. And look at this big tyre tread.'

He sniffs about just like a dog. Soon he is sniffing out onto the road outside. He comes back a minute later and goes over to where the lady is still standing and snuffling. He is holding a wooden chair leg in his hand.

'I'm sorry to say, my dear,' says he, 'that the crunch you heard under the wheel was your father's favourite chair. This is all there is left of it. There are other bits and pieces in the ditch all down the road. I think the men fled in a hurry. I do wonder why.'

He looks at us with his brown round eyes. His eyebrows make little question marks on his forehead. 'We'd best ask Cinnamon,' he says. 'Would you, Cinnamon? A bit of translation for us? Please. We need to understand.'

I had better explain. Talking to animals – easy beasy you will say. Perhaps so. Perhaps. Lots of people talk to animals. They talk to them. They shout at them. They say bad things or good things. Talking is easy. Listening, now that's another thing entirely. Some people can hear us and understand. For them animal talk is clear as clear water. They hear us and they can speak back to us. There are not many people like that. Farmer is one – you may be surprised at that.

But here and now, Cinnamon must do his best and try to tell them what we say. Otherwise Tall Lady and Roly Poly Man will only understand half a word in three, if we're lucky.

Cinnamon walks towards me three careful steps.

I am twitching, tight as a wire. Is this soft creamy mouth the one I'll go down to my own never-come-back? But he stops and sits and curls his luxury tail over his soft round paws and scans all three of us with his crystal eyes.

Woolly Woolly Baa Lamb is up on his feet now. He has stepped forward and the three of us are in a row, me on the front step, Woolly on the gravel path and Cow still lying on the lawn. In fact she's still chewing. Cows get stuck with all this eating. Once they start chewing, chewing is what they do, until all that grass goes down for the second time. What a system, I repeat, but there you go.

'Friends,' says Cinnamon in his soft oil voice. 'There is a story here I do believe. My humans are just a tadge upset about it all. Perhaps you would be so very kind as to tell us what has happened. I imagine,' he says and he nods his head at us very graciously, 'that your own actions were nobility itself. Do tell!'

There is a gleam in his blue eyes. He twitches his tail end just the smallest bit you can imagine. 'Do tell.'

We three look at each other.

'Go on Ratty,' says Cow, 'best talker you are.'

'What about me!' bleats Woolly Woolly Baa Lamb. But I think that Cow is right so I wave my paw at Woolly and get started.

'We were on the track up there,' I say. 'We saw the men taking all the things from the house. We stopped them. It was Cow's idea. We stopped them by spookiness! They ran away!' Cow and Woolly and I all chortle and chuckle at the memory. 'Lovely!' says Woolly. 'Fun!' says Cow.

'I shall tell my humans,' says Cinnamon, 'I shall try to explain. May I enquire – not prying I hope you understand – what you three were doing on the track in the dark time of night, all on your own?'

'I came with my friends,' says I. 'They came because they were heading for never-come-back, the big truck to nowhere. They have numbers you see.' I see him glance over at their two backs. I hope he understands. He turns to me and mouths so that Woolly and Cow cannot see him... 'Lamb chops? Beef stew?' I nod back.

'Miaow!' he says. 'I am proud to meet you. No lying down and taking it like a lamb or like a cow. No indeed. Go for it I say, and you have.' He is quite excited now and upset too. Cool he looks, I think, but not so cool inside.

He sees me think it. He wraps his agitated tail smoothly back over his soft round paws.

'I will explain to them,' he says. He turns to his

humans and in a kind of half talk and half sign language he tries to make them understand. They still look puzzled just a bit, but they smile at us and stretch out hands to pat our heads – Cow's and Woolly's heads anyway.

'Oh,' says the Tall Lady. 'You dear brave things.' She lifts her dainty shoe out of the cowpat and wipes it carefully on a patch of wallflowers – not very happy they look I must say. 'You poor dear things. You brave things.'

'Yes indeed,' says the Roly Poly Man. 'I think you frightened the men away just as they started. You saved our home. Can we help you?'

'Yes,' we all nod but I do not know how they can help us.

Roly Man waves his hand to the house. 'We have to sort out this lot, police, insurance,' he says. 'But first – can we show you our paddock round the back and the stables?'

'That is all very well,' says Tall Lady. 'But I think these are our special friends. They saved our home. Once we are tidy I think they should come inside and be our guests.'

Roly Man gives a sort of squeak. He looks at Cow's big muddy hoofs and at Woolly's sharp wet spikes. He looks into the house. His face is gloomy.

'Anything you say dear,' says he. But I can see he thinks the paddock is a better idea and so do I.

He shows us round to the back of the house.

There is grass and old apple trees. It is very nice indeed. Then Roly Man goes back to the house with Tall Lady and leaves us there. We lie amidst the flowers and gaze up at the sky and eat and doze while police and furniture people and insurance men run around the house and look at the tracks in the driveway and make a lot of noise.

When all the men have gone, Roly Man and Tall Lady come out of the house into the green grass of the paddock. Roly Man looks tired and cross but he smiles when he sees us. 'Come inside and be our guests,' says he.

Tall Lady is brave and kind, but even she thinks our feet need a bit of a clean.

Roly Man cleans Woolly's little hoofs with a wet cloth. Tall Lady puts on a pair of boots and goes to get a hosepipe. Then she sprays Cow's feet. Cow likes this. She whisks her tail and dances up and down.

'Now you are as clean as a whistle,' says Tall Lady, 'and can go anywhere. The Queen would be pleased to have you in her palace,' says she.

I do not know who the Queen is but I bet her palace is no grander than the house we go into now. It is as big as the biggest cow house you have ever seen. Inside it has all separate rooms instead of cow stalls. There is glass in all the windows – just like Farmer's house. On the floor is tufty stuff like grass that smells funny. Cow puts her nose to it and sniffs.

'Not good enough to eat,' says Cow. Woolly shakes his head sadly at that.

There is not much room for Cow, that's for sure. The doorways are very tight and she can't find room to turn round. She parks herself in the hall and waits until we have finished looking round. Woolly does better but he is still too wide. His firm woolly sides are so round and solid that he keeps getting stuck between chairs or behind tables.

I am fine of course. Here and there, upstairs and down, on chairs, up table legs.

'Our house is not a proper animal shape,' says Tall Lady, 'except for you dear Ratty.'

At last we all (except Cow) settle in one room. It is full of round soft chairs to sit on. That suits me but Woolly just stands there. He looks as round and soft as the chairs but crosser.

'We will show you the television,' says Roly Man. He clicks something in the corner. A bright flickery picture shines out at us. I have seen something like this before – through Farmer's window on winter evenings.

We stare. At first we see pictures of people. They are running about and making loud banging noises. Some of them lie down on the ground.

'The News,' says Roly Man. 'It is never good,' he says.

The picture changes. On the flickering screen we

see a truck – it is a sheep truck. We see the thin sheep noses sticking out of the bars. People are trying to stop the truck moving forward. The sheep are calling to us. 'Help!' they bleat. 'Help!'

We all shout together 'Friends! Dear sheep, we will come if we can!'

Cow charges in from the hall. Her eyes are full of tears. We all shout but the animals don't hear us.

'They are a long way off,' says Roly Man. 'That was unlucky,' he says. 'The news is bad for animals too.'

Cow puts her head back and moos so loud that the glass window shakes. Tall Lady puts her hands over her ears.

'I do not think this was a good idea,' says Roly Man.

Cow is stuck. She has her sad face touching the

telly and her big feet jammed between two chairs. There is no hope of her turning round. The sweat is running down her black and white neck. It is very hot in the house.

'You will have to back out,' says Roly Man. He is right.

Up I climb onto Cow's head to help her. Roly Man shouts directions. 'Back a bit – stop there! That way, one step, two. Stop!' It takes a long time but at last Cow is back in the hallway.

Woolly is not happy either. His pale face has gone quite pink under his curls. His little mouth is open and he is panting.

'The house does not suit you too well does it?' says Roly Man. 'Would you rather be outside?'

'Oh yes,' moos Cow. Woolly nods his head. Roly Man opens the front door and Cow goes out backwards. Perhaps a palace is better for cows and sheep. Perhaps Cow could turn round in a palace – but not here.

Woolly skips out. He crashes against a table which gets in his way. There were flowers on the table in a nice bowl but now they are on the ground in a wet mess. Woolly takes a little bite out of one of them. He spits it out. 'Nasty!' says he. 'Smelly and nasty!'

I scuttle out – that is what ratties do.

'We are so grateful to you,' says Tall Lady from

the door. 'Please find any place around the grounds that you like. There is water in the garden – a pond. Just make yourselves at home.'

We find the pond in the shade by the house wall. It is a tiny pond and there are fish in it. The fish don't like it when Woolly scrambles into their water. But Woolly likes it. He stands there for a long time up to his belly in cool water and lilies. He slurps at the water from time to time. The fish don't like that either.

Cow sinks her muzzle into the long green grass by the hedge. I go back to the paddock. I find fallen apples under an old tree and a very dead rabbit by the fence. My sort of thing, you know. May not be your choice but suits me a treat. Cow flops down at last and Woolly comes out of the pond. Three more contented animals would be hard to find.

But we know, here is not the Somewhere we look for. Kind these people are, but this is not our home, our place to be.

'Tomorrow?' says Cow.

'Tomorrow,' I say.

Woolly says nothing because his mouth is full.

We will wait until the morning and then we'll think again.

During that night, I wake. Like the first night. I hear, or seem to hear, a snuffing, a sniffing, a sound of soft paws along the dark road.

I sit up and peer into the dark. For just one moment I think I see a grey shape like a mist passing outside the iron gates. I blink. I know I must be dreaming so I close my eyes once more. When I open them next, I see Tall Lady and Roly Man coming towards us. It is morning and they have breakfast in the pails they carry.

CHAPTER 5

'What you need is a zoo,' says Cinnamon.

Cinnamon and Cow and Woolly and I are all sitting on the lawn in a circle. We are trying to make a plan. 'You need a zoo,' says Cinnamon again.

Zoo is a new word to me, though I am a ratty of the world. 'What is a ZOO?' I ask. I think it sounds a Cow sort of word.

'A zoo,' says Cinnamon, 'is a place where people keep animals. They put them in little concrete squares with wire round them. Or big concrete squares. Or little huts. Then other people come and look at them. And point at them.'

'That does not sound much fun,' says Woolly, 'not so good at all.'

'It is more fun than being on a plate,' says Cinnamon. There is no answer to that.

'Where is the zoo?' I ask.

'There is a zoo in the city,' says Cinnamon. He sees we look puzzled. What is a city we wonder?

'A city is a place where a lot of people live, all together,' he explains. 'We used to live in the city, my two people and me. I have seen the zoo. One day I got up on the high zoo wall and looked in.'

'What is it like?' I ask him.

'It is a big place,' says Cinnamon. 'And there are lots of big animals. Big cats. Big big cats. They call them Lions and Tigers. They are very big indeed. With big teeth.' Cinnamon looks thoughtful.

'Do they have cows in the zoo?' asks Cow.

'Uum,' says Cinnamon, 'they have sort-of cows. With patches and very long necks.'

'I have patches,' says Cow, 'and my neck is quite long.' She stretches her chin up and looks down at Cinnamon.

'Mmmm,' says Cinnamon in a depressed sort of way. 'These cow-things can eat tree tops,' he says. 'They are called Geeraffs I think.'

'Tree tops!' says Cow. 'Oh.' She falls silent and looks glumly at the ground.

'Do they have sheep in the zoo?' asks Woolly.

'Yes they do,' says Cinnamon. He looks at Woolly. 'But not like you. The sheep in the zoo have big horns and jump about a lot.'

'I can do that!' says Woolly. 'I can jump high, so high.' He does, there and then, jumping high on his four hard hoofs. 'But no horns,' he says. He fixes Cinnamon with his little steely eyes.

'No horns,' says Cinnamon and shakes his head.

We all stand silent for a moment. 'So,' says I. 'Zoos is no good. We need something else.'

Even as I speak, Cinnamon's face gets a faraway look and his eyes begin to sparkle.

'I have thought of something,' says he. 'I have not been there but I have heard of it. There is a farm in the city. A special kind of farm. A bit like a zoo. But with cows and sheep and goats and all the animals you are used to. My people have a picture of it somewhere. Wait.'

Off he trots into the house. In a short while he is back, carrying in his creamy mouth a folded piece of paper. He sets it on the ground and flattens it with his chocolate paws. The paper has black dots all over it and a big coloured picture.

'People are funny,' says Cinnamon. 'They love looking at black dots. They call it reading. But the picture is nice isn't it?'

We peer over his shoulder. He is right. There is a picture of a farm, a little farm but a real farm. There are sheep and rabbits and hens and goats and in the corner a brown long face with two curved horns.

'A cow,' says Cow. She smiles so much that her big soft mouth almost reaches her ears. 'A cow. They like cows.'

'And sheep,' says Woolly. 'No horns either. Round and woolly like me.'

There are no rats in the picture. There never are. They are there all the same. People never put rats in a picture but I can almost smell them from here. Behind that food pail. Under that floor. They are there and I would like to meet them.

'Of course,' says Cinnamon in a thoughtful sort of voice, 'it may be that some of these animals go to never-come-back too. It is a farm. But it is a farm for visitors so most must stay around. It is your best chance I think.'

'We will go there,' I say. 'We will go there. We will be safer there, much safer than with Farmer anyway.' Cow and Woolly nod their furry heads and jump a little with joy.

Cinnamon smiles. He waves his elegant tail, slowly and carefully. Then he speaks again. 'It is not so easy,' says he. 'I am sure you are right. It is the best place. But it is not easy to get there. The farm is in the middle of the city. The city is not so far away but it is over a wide river. I know. My people and I crossed the river on a big bridge when we moved here.'

'You crossed a bridge,' I say. I know about bridges.

Farmer has bridges all over his ditches. 'So can we.'

'You could not cross the bridge,' says Cinnamon. 'The bridge is for cars. There is no place for animals. People would stop you. You cannot cross the bridge. You will have to swim.'

We say nothing. We know nothing about swimming, that's for sure.

'I shall have to come with you to show you the way,' says Cinnamon, 'as far as the river at least. I shall tell my people but they may not understand. They will worry of course.' He strokes his soft fur with his chocolate paw. 'They value me highly they do,' says he, and purrs a little. 'They will give me salmon when I get back I am sure.'

So we eat and rest and lie in the sun, while Cinnamon tries to tell his people and hopes they understand.

At last dark night comes. Off we go along the straight track. Off we go, further and further away from Farmer, nearer and nearer to Somewhere.

Cow leads the way. I am high on her head again. Cinnamon sits on her back and shines pale in the moonlight. Woolly trots along behind. I can hear his sharp little hoofs tapping on the muddy track.

Cow is in a frisky mood. She does little dances from side to side and whisks her tail. Cinnamon does not like it. Every time she jumps sideways he sticks his claws in to hang on.

'Stop it!' says Cow. 'That hurts! I do not want holes in my skin.'

Cinnamon looks embarrassed. I do not suppose anyone has told him off since he was a tiny kitten. He jumps down and then he looks at Woolly. 'May I?' says Cinnamon.

'Up you get!' says Woolly. So Cinnamon hops onto Woolly's broad curly back where he can stick his claws in all he likes.

Even I am having a bit of trouble hanging on. Cow is so skippy. I wrap my tail round one curving horn and feel a bit safer.

The moon is rising over our heads when Cinnamon tell us to stop. There is a brightness in the air. Cinnamon says it is the city. He says they have lights on all night in the city. It must be true because there is a great yellow glow in the sky which gets brighter and brighter as we move forward.

'We leave this track here,' says Cinnamon.

We slide down the bank. Cow steps through a broken fence at the bottom of the bank. Woolly pushes after her. Cinnamon and I just hang on tight. Off we go again though it is harder now. The ground is broken and rough. Cow and Woolly go slower. They are careful about their feet.

'Roly Man says this is waste land,' says Cinnamon. 'He does not like it.'

'Not so waste,' says I, 'I can smell flowers. There will be butterflies and birds and crawling things and rats too.'

'True,' says Cinnamon. 'But people like cities better.'

In the glow of the city, we can see the dark river flowing ahead of us. Arching high above is a white and shining bridge. There are lights all along the bridge. From time to time we see smaller lights rushing over it. 'Cars,' says Cinnamon.

Cow steps carefully forward. The dazzle of the city fills the air. Right here, in front of Cow's hoofs, is the river, dark and whispering. It surges away past us towards the high bridge.

'Water!' says Woolly. 'That is nice. I could do with a drink.'

Cinnamon opens his mouth to miaow but Woolly is too quick. He steps up to the water and lowers his mouth. 'Sblaaaaaa!' says Woolly. 'It is salty! Salty! That can't be right!'

'It is true,' says Cinnamon. 'The salt sea is just out there, beyond the bridge. Twice each day it comes up into the river. Then out it goes again. It is going out now,' says Cinnamon, 'but the water will still be salty.'

Woolly shakes his head at the dark water and blinks his fierce blue eyes.

I sit on Cow's head and stare.

I have never seen a river before. It is so big. How can I tell you how big it is?

You know what a road looks like – the road past our farm for one. Think of that road, then two roads side by side, then three, four, five and more again. That is still not wide enough. Even from Cow's head I cannot see the other side.

I can see this side though. The water along the edge goes very slowly and makes little circles by the bank. In the water is a dead rat floating on his back. It is a sad sight. What kind of place is this where a dead rat can float in the grey water and no friend to care? What kind of place indeed. But we are here and have to do what we can.

'You must swim,' says Cinnamon. 'Watch out for boats,' says he, looking up and down the dark river.

'Boats?' says I.

'Boats,' says Cinnamon, 'big floating things. Like water trucks. And big, so big. Watch out,' says Cinnamon.

Never mind boats, I think. First we have to swim. We have seen ducks swim on Farmer's pond. We have seen the young eels swim through Farmer's ditches. But there has been no swimming for us.

'I think I am waterproof,' says Woolly. 'I hope so. But I am not a swimmy shape.' None of us is a swimmy shape – that is what I think.

I once met Otter friend as he bounded his way round Farmer's sheds. He was a swimmy shape. All curvy and bendy and long and strong and covered in thick smooth fur. And he had webbed feet. I look at Cow. And at Woolly. And then down at my round belly and little scratchy paws. We are not swimmy shapes, that is clear – but we can swim if we must. I am sure of that.

Cow steps forward quick and fast into the dark and flowing water. She is up to her knobbly knees in wetness. Cow is a surprise like that. You think she's timid and frightened, and suddenly she's showing the way. A surprising cow is Cow. She is ready to go, with me on her head.

Woolly stares at Cow and takes a step towards the river. Cinnamon leaps down off Woolly's back, very speedy indeed. Woolly doesn't notice. He stares at

Cow so hard with his little steely eyes that his eyes cross.

'Friend Woolly,' says Cow. 'I think you should grab my tail. I am bigger than you. I have bigger legs. If you grab my tail with your tough little teeth you will be towed along. Your head will stay above the water. And we will all get to the other side together.'

Woolly's eyes un-cross. He looks at Cow and he smiles. Woolly doesn't often smile but he does now.

'Friend Cow,' he says. 'You are good to me. I will do that.'

He takes the ragged end of Cow's tail in his tough little teeth. Cow steps forward deeper into the flowing river and Woolly follows.

In no time at all the cold dark wetness is splashing over Cow's big back. We are off. The water is almost up to my claws. I remember that we have not said a proper goodbye to Cinnamon so I turn and wave. He is peering after us and waving his long and chocolate tail. He nods his head to me and watches us until the dark comes down and I see him no more.

The current is strong. I can feel it pushing and pulling Cow's sturdy body.

I look behind us. The current is tugging Woolly so hard that he is not straight behind us but almost sideways. He is a sad sight. The water is splashing over his woolly head. His eyes are shut. I can see his white legs thrashing and thrashing in the water.

The muscles on Cow's back move in big lurches. She swims like she walks. Push one side. Push the other. Strong and swaying. I keep my tail wrapped around me out of the water. I stare at the gleamy water and the stars up above and Cow's nose stretched in front of me.

Above our heads I see the lights of the big bridge and on it the skimming brightness of headlights as the cars rush over it. Nobody knows we are here. That is a good thing, but it will be a bad thing if we sink. Down we will go and no help for it. I am thinking sad thoughts like this when Cow makes a strange noise in her throat. I look forward. I listen.

A thumping thudding noise fills the air. The water ripples and shudders. I look ahead. I look sideways. Cow's ears wave backwards and forwards. And then I see it.

High and heavy, broad and dark. Like the biggest

truck you've ever seen. Ploughing through the water. Moving like a metal wall. Coming towards us. A boat.

It plunges down the river towards the bridge – and straight for us.

Cow lurches sideways. She tries to turn and swim upstream. But the current is too strong. The boat sweeps on towards us.

I look back at Woolly. He cannot see what is happening because his eyes are shut and under water.

'Oh friends,' I whisper, 'is this the end of us?'

The sharp edge of the boat is cutting on towards us. It is going much faster than Cow can swim. If it goes in a straight line it will hit us soon, so soon.

'Oh Cow,' I squeal into her ear. 'Turn round, perhaps the river can save us!'

She has thought of it first. With two big kicks of her back legs she forces her head round again. The current catches her broad side. One more kick and the river picks her up, pushes her, carries her, towards the bridge. As Cow turns, Woolly is pulled over. His little thrashing hoofs show above the dark water. He is almost on his back. I see his tight teeth gripping and gripping for his life. He kicks again. He lifts his wet head as high as he can. He pushes out with his sturdy legs. He has turned, he is right round.

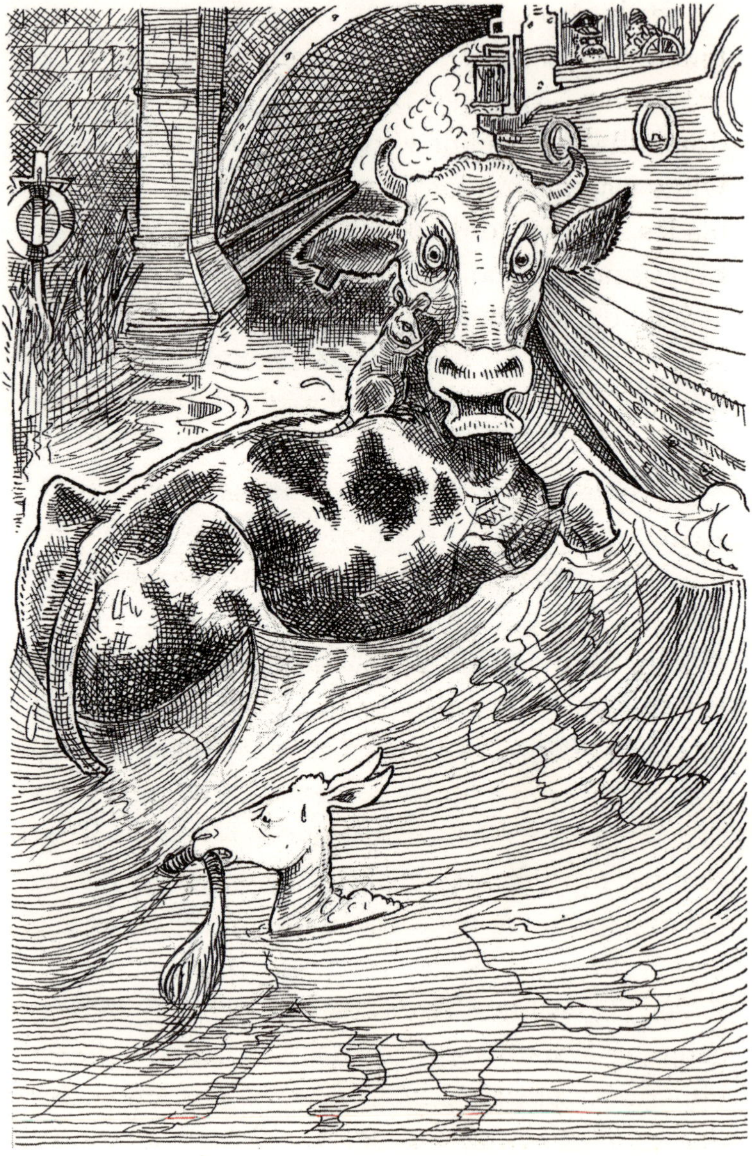

I see his back riding level again. The water seizes him too and rushes us all towards the bridge.

The boat is still there but no closer. We are rushing down the river in line with it. I can see the flurry of white water behind it. I see the silver flash of sharp blades. I sweat to think of them, but they will not hurt us now.

The boat is turning – oh so slightly – but it turns. Away from us and into the deep river centre. It is heading towards the middle of the bridge. With a rush it sweeps under it.

We three float upon the swift water. Cow is hardly swimming now. We float and the river carries us, tugs us on, under the pale arch. We have passed the bridge.

Then Cow turns again. She pushes with her strong legs against the river current. We must still cross the river. We have not begun.

Cow is so brave. I am so proud of her. I beat my tiny feet on her head to tell her. I hope she understands. She turns across the current. The boat is sliding away out of sight, taken by the tide and its own beating engines, to some place I do not know.

Cow kicks out. The water rises up her sides. I cling on. I look back. Woolly is still there. I can hear him snorting through his nose. How far is it? Cow is going slower with every pull of her big legs. We are not swimmy creatures. This is not what we are for.

I peer ahead into the dark. I look up-river and down. Why is it dark? Where is the bright city light? My heart leaps in my wet ratty body. Have we missed the city?

I can still see the bridge. It is on our other side now. Beyond it I see the city glow. But here, as Cow lurches forward, slower and slower through the dark, I see nothing ahead.

The water gets calmer. The pull of the river is less. Cow lifts her head until her mouth is clear.

'Almost there,' she says. I look back. I can just make out Woolly, still holding on. Only his ears are showing above the water, and the tip of his nose. His nostrils open and close just above the dark ripples. River flows over his shut eyes. I see his legs moving steady and firm under the dark water. Woolly is still trying. He has not given up.

We will make it! We are almost there! But where is that?

I stand up tall on Cow's head. I stare ahead. As we get closer I can make out the dark river bank. I see the pale shine of sand in a sheltered bay.

But there is something big and shadowed on the bay shore. I peer harder. Something dark, long, half in the water, half on the dry shore.

At last I see – it is a boat. A big boat, even bigger than the one that almost hit us. It is a boat but it is upside down. Upside down and wrecked and broken and going nowhere. Beyond it I see empty ground, more waste land. Roly Man would not like this.

Cow is moving faster now. Splash, gentle splash goes Cow.

Huff, puff, goes Woolly. His eyes are open now. The water is not so high over his tight little mouth.

Cow steps up and out of the cold river wet. She pulls Woolly up onto the sandy beach. Woolly struggles forward until he can stand too.

Three of us, here, together, safe and over the river.

CHAPTER 6

We are over the river. We are together and safe.

Right in front of us is the high dark shape of the wrecked boat. It looks like a house, a battered rusted house, with a long curved roof. There is a wide and jagged hole in its side – just like a barn door.

'A place to hide. A place to rest,' we all say together.

Cow steps towards it. She pushes her head through the wide door then takes two steps in. I am high on her head, peering up into the dark above. The boat is high and empty and rusted like Farmer's old tractor. A metal cave. The ground beneath Cow's feet is sloping sand piled deep with heaps of weed.

It is quiet inside the dead boat – except for Woolly. He is breathing in a strange rattly sort of way. His head is down at one end and his tail droops at the other. Rattle, rattle. Bubble, bubble he goes, in long panting breaths.

'Oh Woolly,' says Cow, 'are you all right? Can we help you?'

Woolly does not reply. He goes still for a moment. Then he shakes himself. Have you ever seen a wet sheep shake itself? Or a dog even? Or a rat? We all do shaking but sheep do it best. I will tell you how to shake because I know people are not so good at it.

First you plant your four feet solid and square on the ground (or two feet if that's all you've got). Then you pull all your muscles together tight and hard, all crunched up and together. Your shoulders and your back, and your belly up against your backbone, and your bottom and your tail and your neck and your eyes and your whole face. All clenched and tight. And then – you shake. Flick, flack, right, left, faster and faster until all you see is a blur in front of your eyes and your head rings and hums. Then you stop. And watch the water from your coat fly into the air and fall to the ground.

We can all shake – but sheep do it best.

Woolly shakes now. His thick white wool spins

back and forth in front of us. His head disappears into a blur. Water drops fly in a bright mist high into the air. They catch the dazzle of the bridge lights. They shine like diamonds and glow like rainbows. They hang about him so that he is a sheep in a halo.

Then the mist falls to the ground and joins all the other wetness. He is Woolly, back to his normal curly self.

But his breath still rattles.

So now he coughs.

Rats don't cough. Cows cough sometimes. Sheep cough and a hard nasty sound it is. Woolly stretches out his pale neck and his hard little chin. He closes his eyes and coughs as if he wants his insides to come to the outside. Cough, heave, cough, heave. We see bits of spray and tiny flecks of muck and dirt shoot out of his mouth, and out of his slanty nostrils. One cough. Two coughs. Three. Then silence. Woolly waits a moment. He pulls his head in with a little wiggle and turns to Cow.

'That's better,' he says. 'I am fine now. I was a bit worried for a while. I am not so waterproof as I thought. But I am fine now.'

Fine he says. But how fine is this? That is what I think. We three. Together yes. In a dark cave of metal while the wind blows loud outside. Fine? Well maybe. That's what I think.

Perhaps Woolly thinks the same. He looks up into

the dark roof above us. His face is pale and tired. 'We are safe now,' says he, 'but I cannot live in a boat. I need fields and friends and a farm.'

Cow turns her head and listens to the wind blowing on the metal walls. I can hear the water drip drip from her wet body onto the wet sand. We are a long way from fields and friends and farms now.

Then my round ratty ears catch a faint hiss above my head. Above my head. Then behind me. Then from the metal walls. Louder. Louder. Until the air sings around us.

Woolly goes stiff with fright. He has swum the river but he doesn't like hisses from nowhere.

'What is that?' says he. 'Who's there?'

And from the midst of the hiss, high and faint, I hear 'Usssss. Usssss.'

Woolly is getting cross now. He is too tired and wet to play games.

'Well who is Uss? That's what I want to know,' he bleats loud and cross. And then he stamps his hard hoof.

'Ouch!!' goes a hissing squeak from below us. 'Almossst got me that time he did! Watch out friends! He's got nassty sharp things on his feet. Really nassty!'

'Nasty! Nasty! Nasty!' chant a hundred whispery voices all around us.

Woolly's eyes flash. 'I swim a river,' he snorts through his damp white nose, 'I swim a river and what do I find on the other side! Bad manners!' says he. 'Rudeness!' says he. 'And...' he opens his mouth to say more. Then he shuts it again.

His white woolly face goes quiet. He is thinking hard. He has remembered the rhyme. The whole rhyme. There is no water in his brain, that's for sure.

> *'Hoof or paw,*
> *Tame or free,*
> *Under the fur,*
> *Friends are we,'*

says Woolly proudly.

Well that's all very well, but will it work? That's what I ask myself. It doesn't sound quite right to me. And anyway, it is a doggo rhyme – and whatever these voices are I do not think they are doggos.

'Hoof! Paw! What's he talking about?' mutter voices above us.

'Fur! Under the fur! Yuuk! How disgusting!' say voices by our feet.

'Land talk. Dry talk,' mutter a thousand tiny voices from the metal walls around us. 'No good to us, that's for sure. Sea talk, that's what we want! Wet talk.'

Woolly looks worried. He doesn't know what to say next.

My eyes are getting used to the flickering shine from the river. I stare around me. The metal curves are covered with shells, and between the shells are soft jelly flowers. I clutch Cow's ear and peer upwards. Each shell has a little roof on it, I see, half open now. And the jelly flowers wave and nod.

'Are you uss?' I whisper into the dark roof space.

'Yess,' they whisper back. 'But who are you?'

'We are dry land things,' says I, 'but wet. We have swum the river.'

'We need shelter,' says Cow. 'Can we rest here? The wind is so cold.'

'Yes, yes, s'pose so, all right then,' say all the tiny voices. 'But why are you here? Where are you going? Tell us! We have time and to spare. It is a long wait for the tide.'

'We are going to the city,' says I from Cow's head, 'to the farm in the city, to be safe.'

'Ssafe. Ssafe,' they whisper. 'That sounds good.

But we cannot help you. Not us. We know nothing. Except the river water. We cannot help you.'

'If we can stay and hide here, that is help indeed,' says Cow. She is polite even when she is cold.

'But not enough,' bleats Woolly. His face is pale and tired. 'We need a friend to show us our way.'

'You need a furry running thing,' says one voice braver than the rest. 'There is only one such on this shore. You need Shell Eater.'

A tremble of sound hisses through the dark hollows of the boat. 'Shell Eater!' a thousand voices whisper. 'May the tide protect us,' they say soft and low.

Then on the night wind it comes. A sound. From far away.

Cow turns her great ears. I lean my head and listen. Through the bluster of the wind on the high boat roof, we hear a voice. Singing. High and far away.

Far away. Faint. Then closer.

'It is she!' hiss the shell voices. 'Shell Eater is here!'

The voice floats clearer to us now. And then the words hit my ear.

>'Shells and fisshes,
>So delisshus!'

chants the voice, high and happy and fierce.

'Shells and fisshes,
Quite delisshus!'

The voice is closer now. Cow turns and steps back to the high doorway. She pushes her head out into the night air. I hang on tight to her ears and look along the gleaming shore.

I see a shadow on the sand. A curving leaping bouncing shadow. A creature, a four-legged furred thing, like you and me. Plain as plain. Bounding along the shore and singing as she comes.

She leaps and curves like Otter but she is smaller than he, and darker. Her tail is wide and bushy like Fox's own. The cold moon gleams on her dark fur.

'Mink!' says I. People wrap themselves in that fur I have heard tell. 'Mink.'

She is heading for the boat.

Cow steps out into the moonlight. The bounding creature leaps once more. 'Quite delisshus!' she cries. She skips with joy. And then she sees us.

She stops so quick that her four paws make little fountains of sand.

'Oh my,' says she. 'Oh my!'

She sits back and stares. And stares again.

'A cow. And a sheep,' she says. 'Are you real? Or am I dreaming?'

'Real enough,' says I from my high perch.

She has not seen me. She gives a little scream and

tumbles flat on her back in the wet. She stares up at me.

'I am Ratty,' says I. 'These are my friends, Cow and Woolly.'

She bounds up onto her four feet with a flash of dark fur. Her pointed face peers up at me. Her eyes gleam like wet pebbles.

'I am Minka,' says she. 'This day is too much for me! Strangeness on strangeness! I have lived on this grey shore for two summers and two winters. I have never seen a cow or a sheep in all that time. Nor yet a man and a dog. So please explain dear Ratty if you can.'

I do not like the sound of the man and the dog. But I tell our tale. I tell our story, from the first running out of Farmer's farm, to the spooking at the house, the long walk to the river, and the great river crossing.

I tell it loud and clear from Cow's high head as the night wind blows. I know the shell things hear me too.

'We need the city farm,' I say when I have told all, 'and soon. My friends are weary to the bone. They cannot go much further.'

'The City Farm?' says Minka. 'I do not know it. But I know the city, who does not?'

'Take us to the city,' says Woolly. 'Be our friend in this.'

Minka sets her head on one side. She scratches her ear with a dark front paw. 'I could,' says she. 'I will. But you do not know the worst.'

My blood runs cold at that. What does she mean?

'There is a hunter on the shore,' says she.

Cow and Woolly lift their tired heads and stare at her. 'A hunter?' says Woolly.

'There was a man, by the river side, when the moon was rising,' says she. 'And a big dog with him. Men do not go there, nor dogs neither. Not in the dark time. They were hunting,' says she. 'That is for sure. I know hunting when I see it.'

'Maybe so,' I say. The cold wind ruffles my fur. I shiver. 'Maybe so.'

She looks up at me with her shiny pebble eyes. 'Hunting for you?' she asks. 'For your friends?'

I look down at her. I nod my head slow and quiet. 'I fear it,' I whisper.

Cow and Woolly have other things to think about. They are tired of standing on this windy shore. They are hungry.

Cow lifts her head. 'I can smell grass,' says she.

Woolly lifts his wet white nose and sniffs. 'You are right,' he says. 'Dear Cow you are right again. Grass is close by. Let us look – let us sniff it out. We herbivores must stick together. Eating comes first.'

Minka looks up at me. Her eyes are round with surprise. 'But they are hunted,' she whispers. 'How can they eat? How can they think of eating?'

Cow and Woolly are not listening. Sniffing and sniffing Woolly walks step by step up the wet mud bank. A few paces further and he gives a wild and joyous bleat.

'Here! Cow! Grass! Oh joy!' He falls silent but we can hear the brisk chop chop of his teeth.

Cow turns and almost staggers up the slope. She leans her long neck forward. With a great clunk her teeth tear at a long shoot of grass. I slide down her neck and leap out onto the cold ground.

'It is eating time,' I say to Minka, 'and that is that.'

I am the hungriest rat this side of the river. I am cold and weak and not the rat I like to be. We have swum the wide river in the cold dark. We have thought that never-come-back may be the salt sea and us in it. That is a hungry feeling.

'It was eating time for me, too,' says Minka, 'before I saw you three upon the beach.' She looks at the dark boat shape. She licks her lips. 'Shells are tasty,' says she.

I shake my head. 'The shell folk have been our friends,' says I.

'Oho,' says she. 'Eating friends is not so nice. Not so nice.' She gives the boat a last sad look. Then she shakes her deep fur from tail to nose and leaps to her feet.

'I'll go and hunt,' says she, 'and be ready for the morning when it comes. Not a good morning, no, I think not,' she mutters, 'not good.' And off she skips into the night.

I take my own way along the shore line. Ratties can always find something. Smelly things, strange things, leftover things. All fine for a ratty stomach.

Cow and Woolly munch on. We three eat until our sides swell out and our faces smile again. That is an hour or two or perhaps more. Then we raise our heads and sniff about us. We need shelter. So back we go to the dark boat on the shore.

From deep in the dark comes a whisper of shell talk. 'Is she there? Did you find her?'

'Oh yes,' says I, 'we met Shell Eater. And she will help us to the city. She is hunting now but she will come here soon.'

'Sssooooon.' There is a shuddering whisper from the shells. 'She will come sssooooon?'

'Soon and now!' calls a voice from behind us. There is a scatter of sand against the metal wall of the ship. Before I can catch breath, here she is.

Minka. Shell Eater. Her fur gleams in the half light. She stares up at the shell things where they cling to their narrow ledges. A silence falls so deep that I can hear my own heart beat within my ratty chest.

Minka stares up at the shell things. Her whiskers twitch and sparkle in the river light. She licks her lips. But then she shakes her head. And sits back upon the sand.

'You are safe,' says she at last. 'I cannot eat the friends of my friends.'

The silence holds a moment. Then a high hiss starts as we first heard it. Faint and then growing louder and louder until our ears hum.

'Welcome back,' say the high shell voices. 'We are glad,' they whisper, 'glad that you found someone to guide you. She knows the city and we do not. Come in,' they say, 'and rest.'

Cow steps forward very carefully on her big feet. Woolly shuffles after her. He is weary. So are we all. It has been a long time since we last lay down and shut our eyes.

Cow finds a dry corner. She settles down onto the ground. Soon Woolly goes down too. They look like pale stones in the river light.

Minka leaps back into the high doorway. She leans against the cold metal. She keeps watch upon the long shore line.

I find a pile of wet weed and tuck my head down

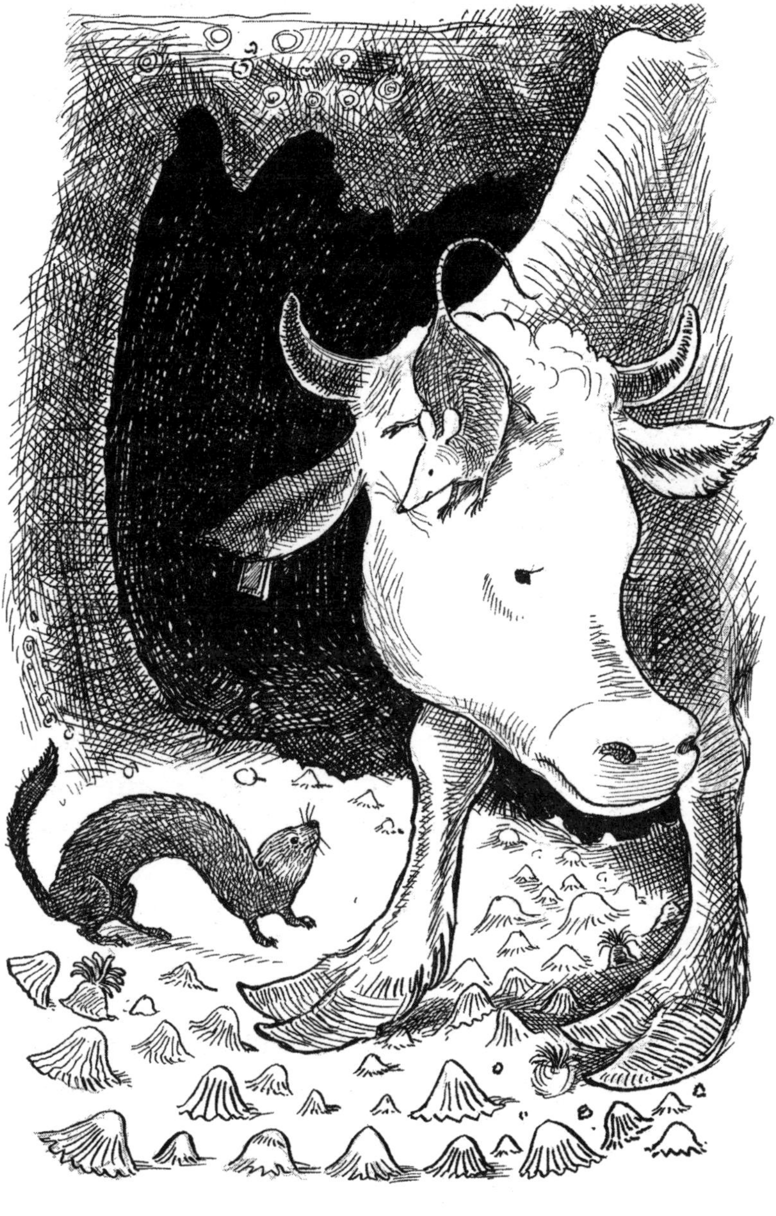

onto my fat warm belly. As I drift off I hear Cow's jaws clunk clunk in the night and Woolly's little breaths come thick and fast from his tired chest. I see Minka's dark shape in the doorway.

No snuffing and sniffing this night. Not here. Not now. But I remember Minka's words and shudder. Then I sleep – like a rat who has crossed a wide river and lived.

I sleep. But suddenly I am awake. Wide awake in the cold first light of morning.

'Get up,' says the hiss of voices. 'Get up on your legs, land things. Move or swim.'

I look about me. I squeak with terror. The water! What has happened to the water? It is lapping right up to my weed bed. It washes against my scaly tail. 'The river has come to get us!' I squeak. 'We are doomed!'

I squeal and squeal and pull my tail out of the lapping river. I am not very sensible first thing in the morning or very brave either.

'The tide! The tide!' sing the tiny shell voices. 'It brings us food. Food, and sea talk and cool wetness. Oh happy tide.'

They like it. And Minka, too. I see her out along the shore, leaping through the ripples of the high water. They like it but not us. For me and Woolly and Cow, it is more wetness than we want.

'We must go,' says Cow. 'Get up Woolly! Get up!'

Woolly opens his eyes. He sees the water. He blinks twice. Then up he gets on his four hard hoofs.

'Water!' says he. 'No more water! Dry land is best and dry sheep are better.' He does not wait but trots off, out of the doorway and up the narrow beach.

Then he stops and turns.

'Thank you, wet folk,' says Woolly. 'I shall remember you.'

'Thank you indeed,' says Cow. And she too steps out onto the beach.

I scurry after them. I pause in the doorway and look back into the gloom. The water is high now. The boat is almost full. The ripples lap against the cold and rusted walls.

'This is your tide,' say the voices. 'Go now!'

'Goodbye friends,' I say.

Then off I scamper up the cold grey morning shore. I scramble up Cow's leg onto her tall shoulder. I hunch my shoulders against the wind. It is morning and we must find the city.

CHAPTER 7

We stand on the grey shore and look about us. What next?

Minka comes leaping through the ripples towards us.

'The city is that way,' says she, 'beyond the bridge. But there is danger.' She stands tall on her back legs and peers and sniffs the air.

'I smell hunting,' she says. 'You must find a place to hide. I need to plan a way into the city. That is hard for big things like you. So you must hide. But you are so big, so big! Where can you hide in this flat place?' She hisses between her sharp teeth. 'Where?' says she.

Cow and Woolly look at the bridge. Then at each other, a question in their eyes.

'There,' says Cow.

'Under the bridge,' says Woolly.

Minka turns and stares at the bridge.

It shines bright in the morning light. Along the river edge beneath it, there is a thin strip of dry ground.

'We could hide there,' says Cow. 'For a while.'

'You could,' says Minka slowly, thinking as she speaks. 'The city is that way too. You would be one step on your way.'

'It will do for now,' says Cow. 'The light is rising. We cannot stand here.'

'You are right,' says Minka. Her pointed face is anxious. 'It will do for now. You will be safe from eyes upon the bridge. But it is no shelter from the hunters. Not if they come by the shore.'

'If they hunt us they will find us,' says Cow. 'There is no help for that.'

Minka stares and then at last she nods her head. She lifts her nose and sniffs the air. Then she starts off towards the bridge.

'I'll show you the best way,' says she. 'Big-foot cow and tubby sheep need an easy path.'

Woolly stamps his little feet and snaps his blue eyes. He snorts but there are more important things to do than be cross. He knows that.

'This way is best,' says Minka.

She leads us up a long slope of rough bare ground towards the bridge.

The bridge is high above us. There may be eyes up there and if there are, what can we do?

We take a little turn, up and then down again. We go by smooth grass to the very riverside. Now the bridge is like a roof over our heads. We stand upon a square of dry earth. The river runs by and the river wind blows over us.

It does not feel safe. No one above can see us that is true. But what if someone comes along the shore? No help for it, as Cow has said.

Minka sits by Cow's feet. She darts her head this way and that.

'It does not feel right,' says she. 'This morning early, I heard an engine noise. From this waste land. A loud noise, like a van. But who would bring a van up here? Who?'

'And why?' says I, although I think I know.

'It could be the Scientist, I suppose,' says Minka. 'But why so early? She never comes so early.'

'Who is the Scientist?' I ask.

'She comes here often,' says Minka. 'She, and some others too. They look after the river – that is what they say. I have heard them. They look at the water and put it in tubes. Very odd,' says Minka.

I have a cold feeling in my heart. Farmer has many friends I know. Perhaps the Scientist is one of them.

Then Cow lifts her head. She stares along the grey line of the river shore. 'Someone is coming,' she says.

Right she is. A woman has stepped into view, round the bend of the river. 'It is her. It is she!' cries Minka. 'Oh what shall we do now?'

Nothing – is the answer to that. There is nothing we can do. There is nowhere to run to and we are not good runners anyway. The woman sees us. She waves. We do not wave back.

She trots towards us. She scrambles along the shore to where we stand and here she is.

She is thin and small and her hair is red. She has a sharp sort of face, a bright sort of face, with white white teeth. I look at her and wonder where I have seen that kind of face before. And then I remember. She has a face like a weasel. A weasel face is good on a weasel, none better, but not so good on a person.

You may not know what a weasel is like. You may never see a weasel, not in all your life. Ten times out of ten they see you first and off they go. Weasels are thin and red and quick, so quick. And fierce. Good folk they be, I don't say otherwise. Brave and clever and never-give-up. But would I trust a little ratlet to a weasel? I think not. Especially if that weasel was hungry. And this weasel woman looks as if she has been hungry all her life.

'I have come to help you,' says she.

Help us? We say nothing.

'I saw your tracks by the river,' says she. 'I heard talk last night that there were farm creatures straying hereabouts. That is not right you know. Wild places for wild things, I say. You should not be here.'

I do not like this. And what does she mean she has heard talk? Who is talking? Where? This is bad indeed.

'I have guessed where you are heading,' says she. 'There is just one place for cows and sheep in this big city,' says she, 'except the place you know of – and no one heads there on their own four feet!'

She laughs. It is not a nice noise. High and sharp and more weaselish than ever. Weasels love blood, that is the truth, and perhaps she does too. 'You want the farm in the city,' says she. 'Am I right?' She looks at us and we look back.

Woolly nods his curly head very very slowly. He looks like a beaten lambkin and so say all of us I think.

'I thought so,' says she. 'I have a van,' she says, 'I can take you there. I love animals,' says she, 'I do indeed. I will help you.'

Woolly looks at me. His eyes are pale and wintry bright. Cow turns her dark glance on me too. As for me? What do I feel? I feel as if I have fallen into cold cold water. But I am thinking just a bit. Perhaps the fright has not frozen my brain all up yet.

'Let us consider, friends,' I say to Cow and Woolly. I notice that Weasel Woman does not seem to understand. So she does not talk Animal. She loves animals but does not understand us. More bad news.

'We can go with her or we can stay.'

'Yes,' they nod.

'We have a choice.' They nod. 'I will tell you what that choice is.'

They wait and listen but they know it already.

'To go with her is full of danger.'

'Yes,' they nod.

'To stay means death. People will find us. Farmer will be told. Death, certain death. It is risk to go but death to stay.'

They look at me and I at them. They are my friends and this is our choice. It is a choice easy made. Easy to make. Hard to do. They nod their heads. I nod mine. Minka behind me shivers. She is silent. She wants no part in this.

We turn back to Weasel Woman. She is still standing there. She has keys in her hand and is jangling them and looking out over the river.

'Ready?' she says.

We nod. She turns and trots back the way she came, on her two thin legs. We trot after her, Woolly and Cow and me up on Cow's head. Minka runs after us with a sad and worried face, like a friend who is saying the longest goodbye of all.

The sun has risen full and bright. We feel the warmth on our backs. I look up behind me and yes, people do see us. Someone in uniform is peering over the bridge above us. I see him give a little start and wave to someone else to come and look. We had only one choice indeed and this is it.

Weasel Woman leads us off along the rough shore. In a few steps we reach a road with grass growing through it. On we trot and round the corner we find the van. Just as she said.

It is green, shiny, and square like a box. It has a big truck door that comes down on the road. Just like a cow truck, or a sheep truck for that matter.

'Oh no,' says Cow. 'It is a cow truck, whatever it looks like. I can't Ratty. Not a truck. No!'

All her black and white body begins to shake and tremble. Even her thick flat knees knock a bit. 'Oh Ratty. Can it be safe?' she asks. 'It can't be. This is a trap.'

I can feel her cold panic sweat rising round my feet.

'It may be,' I say. 'It may be. But how else can we travel? We must get through the city. We have been seen already I fear. Soon we will be chased by Farmer and those like him. This is our only way.'

Woolly's steely little eyes are crossed with fright. 'I's a brave sheep,' he says, 'tough as a woolly can be, but Ratty, to step into a truck, walk into a truck! How can I?'

'We have to be braver still, Woolly,' I say. 'We have come so far together. Let us go on, frightened though we be.'

But they take more risk than I do, and they know it. A ratty can leap and flee and hide, and be away in a minute. Cows and sheep are big and slow and take their time. They are right to tremble.

Weasel Woman goes round to open the big back door. She unlocks the bolts, one on each side and one at the top of the door. She loosens a final toggle at the top. She lets the door down slowly into a ramp.

She turns and waves us in. She wants us to step up that steep ramp, into that dark box, the way so many of Cow's friends and Woolly's friends have gone before them.

Cow is trembling and Woolly too but they are as brave as brave can be. They step up that ramp into that dark truck space. They do it. I scramble up after them. I haul myself up Cow's tail and run up onto her head, looking at nothing in particular because it is so dark.

When the big back door is closed shut, it is as dark as a barn at night, or the inside of Doggo's kennel. I shiver, but we are all in this together so I pat Cow's head with my paw. Cow rubs her big head against Woolly's curly flank. We do our best to be brave and cheerful. The engine starts up and the van begins to lurch forward.

There is a narrow window high in the van's side. I stand on Cow's head and peer out.

I see Minka. Waiting on the road edge. Sad and quiet. She is still as still can be. Suddenly she leaps to her feet. She stands up tall on her back legs. She stares. At what? She is staring down the road, in front of the van. At what?

My heart shakes in my body.

The truck stops again. Our driver opens her door. What is going on?

'Just a helping hand,' Weasel Woman calls back to us in the back. 'A bit of company.'

There is a scrabbling noise but no words, no words at all. What kind of helping hand is this? What kind of company? I cannot see from where I am but my blood is running thick and cold.

I look back at Minka. She is on her four feet again now. Her thick tail is arched rigid and high. Her sharp white fangs are bared and snarling. 'Danger! Danger!' she says with every hair and every whisker. As if I haven't guessed. 'Oh Ratty,' her rigid fur tells me, 'oh Ratty brother, watch out! Keep those sharp little wits about you!'

I see the message. I fear the worst.

'What's up Ratty?' says Cow. 'I cannot see out. What is happening?'

'What's up Ratty?' asks Woolly. 'We've stopped already. Is it a plot? Are we going to never-come-back, after all?' And he butts his poor panicking head against the side of the truck once, twice, three times.

'Friends,' I say, 'all may be well. We will be ready for anything that comes our way. And anyway, we are off again now.'

So we are. The engine roars again, the van lumbers off down the bumpy road and we have started the next long step to Somewhere.

Or so I hope.

I press my little paws together and think of Minka's snarling frightened eyes.

CHAPTER 8

What a truck this one is!

I remember the trains, the people trucks that Doggo told us of. Glass, he said, along the side so that people can see out as they go. That would be nice. I'm sure people don't all stand crammed up together and lean on each other at every bend as we do now.

Cow is standing in one corner of the van, behind a high board up to her shoulder. I suppose it is to stop her toppling to the floor. Woolly just stands. Perhaps Weasel Woman thinks he is so short and padded that he will not hurt himself, bounce though he may. He is not best pleased though. Every time we stop suddenly, which is more often than you would think, he bumps his nose on the front wall or bounces off the door behind.

'Baaah!' says Woolly. 'Never mind the journey's end, this journey's not a lambkin's dream, I can tell you. What are people thinking of?' he says. 'No sheep sense at all.'

We bounce on over rough ground for a while and then it gets smoother. We can hear the throb and roar of other cars and vans outside. The air is warmer now.

'We need a window open,' says Weasel Woman, 'I'm all in a sweat here.' We hear her slide her window down.

'I suppose you animals would like some air too,' she says and she pushes back a sliding panel between us and the cabin. A cooling flood of air whisks over us. We breathe deeper.

Suddenly the truck gives a lurch. It goes up, shakes, and then crashes down again. Over a bridge I think. Cow's head shoots up and up I go.

For a moment I am up in the air, hanging in mid-air, gripping with my paws and hoping for the best. High up, for that brief moment, I see down past our driver's red hair and thin shoulders, into the cabin.

There, next to our driver, I see an ear, two ears, two grey ears. Someone is sitting in the passenger seat, and that someone is a doggo. A grey doggo. A big grey doggo with fluffy ears.

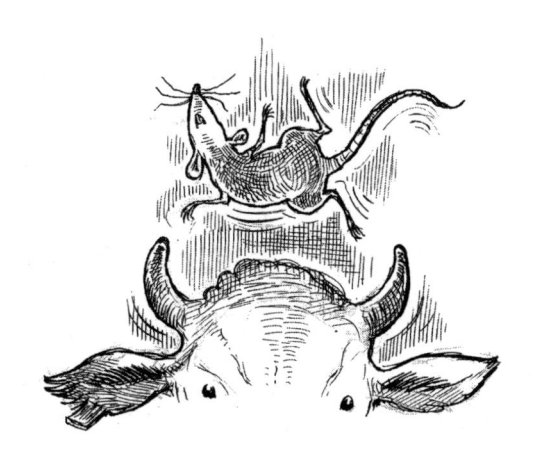

'All right are you Ratty?' asks Cow. 'Your claws are gripping a bit tight there.'

'Sorry Cow,' I gasp. 'Shaken up a bit that's all. Fine now,' but my squeak trembles.

I cover my eyes with my paws. It is Wall-Eyed Doggo, the Farmer's Friend. His grey doggo mind is full of some plan I am sure and it is not to make us happy. Oh no. I shake my head and whimper in my throat. Quiet though I am, Cow hears me and her anxious voice rises from below me in the half light.

'Sure you're all right there, Ratty?'

'I'm fine, Cow,' I say. Truth is, I may be. Farmer doesn't want me back. Oh no. Doggo will have his work cut out driving Cow and Woolly. He won't want me around. I am free now and I'll stay that way. But my friends! I bury my long brown nose in my paws and cry as quietly as I am able. This time Cow doesn't notice.

We bump on. The van lumbers round corners and sways along the straight sections but at last there are signs of a change.

'Almost there,' says Weasel Woman. She slows the van to a halt. I peer out of the high window and see that we are at a crossroads. She leans her head out of her window for a moment.

'You said to stop here didn't you?' she says to silent Doggo. 'This is the place? Ah yes – I can see him. George!' she shouts. She waves her arm in the air. Then she pulls her arm back. The engine roars louder. She takes the van round the corner, slower and slower until at last it stops, in some kind of yard. She opens her door and skips out.

Cow and Woolly prick up their ears. They stand as still as stone and sniff the air.

'I can't smell farm,' says Cow in a strange faraway voice. 'No farm here Ratty.'

'No farm here,' says Woolly, 'no farm here but cars and people and lots of house smells, like Farmer's house, lots of them and...' He sniffs on. His ears shoot straight up above his head. He turns his pale blue eyes to me and they are empty as a winter sky.

'Farmer,' he says very low, very quiet. 'I smell Farmer and I smell Wall-Eyed Doggo too.'

Cow is shaking under my feet. She is sniffing the air but no need for sniffing. Here is the door thrown open. The light of bright day breaks in upon us, and there below us stand Farmer and his Wall-Eyed Friend.

We look down at them and a sorry sight we must be. Three broken hearts in a row.

'Doggo,' I say, 'we trusted you.' I have more voice than the others but then I have more life ahead of me.

'Sorry Ratty,' says Doggo, but he doesn't look very sorry to me. 'You know how it is. Doggos have to be loved. You know that. I want to be Farmer's Friend, that is best of all. And now I am Farmer's best friend, I am, I am.'

He wags his doggo tail and presses his nose against Farmer's leg. Farmer pats his grey head and turns to Weasel Woman.

'Thanks a lot,' says Farmer. 'Good thing I bumped into you when I did. This dog, you wouldn't believe what this doggo has done,' says Farmer. 'When these two animals ran off,' (he doesn't mention me you will notice – losing a rat off his farm doesn't get him much sympathy, I suppose) 'they just vanished, no trace at all. But this dog tracks them down. How he did it I don't know. He found them. Then he comes back to me. The rest is history as they say. What a doggo!'

Farmer is very pleased with Doggo, that is plain enough. Weasel Woman bends and pats his head. He puts up with it bravely. Perhaps he does not know what she is like.

'I've got a new pup,' Farmer says to Weasel who is not looking too interested. 'Good breeding, best stock. Not a patch on this one, though. Never will be. Can't beat experience I say.' He pats Doggo's head like he's giving out medals. Doggo looks like doggos do at times like this, smug.

'Well,' says Weasel Woman, 'I remember how you always were George. Like to keep what's yours, whatever it costs. Talking of which...' says Weasel Woman.

'Yes indeed,' says Farmer. 'I had not forgot. Come into this pub with me,' says Farmer, 'and I'll see you right. As for this lot,' and he points at us, 'I'll give old Mac a buzz and he can take them now. They'll be mutton and beef in two hours! They've just come a long way round!' He laughs the kind of laugh you never want to hear, my friends.

'Shut that door up,' says Farmer to Weasel. 'I'll make that call and we'll settle up. What do they mean, scarpering off like that!' Farmer is still angry that is clear. 'Animals!' says he. 'Who'd have 'em!'

Weasel shoves the door back up and slips the bolts across with a flick of her hand. We are in the dark again. We hear their feet, clomp, clomping off into the pub.

'Ah Ratty,' says Cow into the silence. 'A good run we made but nothing to do now. All over now. Shut-our-eyes-and-wait time now.'

But I have had my microsecond, my minute to think and I am not beaten yet. Clever finkers we are, us ratties, and I see a way. A hopeless way of course, but a way to try at least.

'Cow,' I say. 'Please Cow. Do not give up. Not yet. There may be a way.' She looks up at that. She has great faith in me I see. I feel my heart turn over. I just hope she is right.

'A way?' she says. She opens her trusting eyes

wide and stares at me. Woolly stops butting his head against the door and stands very very still.

'Yes,' I say. 'I've been looking at this door. I think that our Weasel lady has done a sloppy job this time. Look. There are three bolts – you can see the screws on the inside. There's one on each side and one at the top. Then there is the toggle catch at the top, a sort of safety catch. When we were travelling they were all locked. Not now. She just pushed the toggle in and slipped the bolts across. Then off she went with Farmer. So perhaps, perhaps, we have a chance.'

'But how Ratty?' says Cow. 'The bolts are all on the outside and we are on the inside. Sorry,' she says, 'you know that.'

'You are on the inside,' says I, 'but I can get out as quick as you can say Ratty.' And I show her. I jump up from her high head and skip out through the narrow window onto one of the wooden struts that seem to run all round the van sides. Out I slip. Then I pop straight back and look down at Cow and Woolly.

'You see,' says I, 'I can climb out easy beasy like this. I'll go round the back to where the door opens. If this strut goes all the way round I can perch on it. Then I can reach two of the bolts at least. I can push at them – I'm strong you know, though they are heavy bolts.'

I am trying to think it through. 'Perhaps it would help if the door was shifted up a bit, and pulled in a bit too. Yes,' I say, 'if you, Cow, could get your shoulder to this handle and just lift it a bit... yes that's right. And look, Woolly, if you could put your tight teeth into that rope, the one that is hanging from that hook on the inside, and pull back when I say the word – well, then I think the bolts might be easier to shift. I might have a fair chance then.'

'Oh Ratty,' says Cow, 'of course I can do that.' Woolly is a lamb of action and he has already seized the rope in his white mouth and is ready for the heave.

'Wait,' I say, 'let me climb out again and see what's what.'

So back I go, through the window and into the outside world. And there I stop and look about me, dumbstruck. I am looking out into a world like nothing I have seen before.

CHAPTER 9

I crouch there, high on the van side. My eyes are blinking. I am dazzled.

It is so bright. It is so noisy. There are more people here than I have ever seen in my whole life, just here, all in one view from this van.

We are parked in the corner of a flat square space. It is full of cars. People are everywhere. There are people in the cars, people walking, people standing. There are children, and men, and women, and dogs, and one black cat. The cat is looking at me with green and popping eyes from a fence a short way off. Lots of the people are pushing silver carts. Some of them are feeding their cars with food from the carts. My ratty mouth is open wide with astonishment. What is this?

'This is something new,' I say to myself, 'this must be the city.' You will remember that I have been to a town, once, so I know what I am talking about.

Then I give my whiskers a sharp tug. 'What are you thinking of boy,' I say to myself, 'there is work to do here.'

I edge round the corner of the van and see that luck is on our side. The strut that I am standing on runs right on across the back door, under the two side bolts. I shall have firm standing when I pull those bolts, or push them or something... I am not clear yet so I take a look at the nearest one.

I give it a pull. No, that won't do. It doesn't move at all. My paws are just not right for this work. I scuttle to the other end of the bolt. I put my shoulder to it and push instead. Better.

'Now,' I hiss through the door. Cow pushes her great shoulder upwards and Woolly must be throwing himself backward with all his curly weight because the door shifts up, and inwards. The bolt moves just a bit, under my shoulder. I push with all my ratty strength. I close my eyes and grit my long rat teeth.

'Again,' I hiss and the bolt gives and slides along its groove. This side is free.

'Good work,' I whisper through the gap in the door. 'Now for the other side.'

I scuttle across and get my shoulder to the second bolt. It is even harder to shift. But I heave and push and we do it again.

The sweat is running through my fur now. I have a kind of mist in my eyes. Ratties are not made for hard work, not heavy work. We are not your weightlifters, your tough guys. More your wheeler-dealers really. But I am a round ratty, fat some say, and every mouthful that has made me round and glossy helps me now.

There is only one bolt left and that is at the door top. The bolt goes upwards into the edge of the roof, right in the middle.

I leave my strut and scamper up the van side onto the top. This bolt is not so easy. A good heave will not fix this one. It is turned sideways. If I can twist it, it will drop, down and out of the round clips on the frame above. How can I do that?

I peer over the roof of the van. I shall have to lean right out to push the bolt round. When I stretch like that my paws aren't very strong. What can I do? I scratch my brown and furry brow.

'Need a hand mate?' says a small voice at my back. I spin round quick as a flash and just about fall off doing it. I do not expect a voice up here I can tell you, and I don't see who it is for a moment. Then I look down behind me.

It is a mouse. Very small, very weedy-looking, with a smile and a twinkling eye.

'Could do with a hand, mate?' says she quick and twangy. 'Takes two I believe this kind of thing.'

'Well friend,' I say, 'if you know how to do this, you are a good friend to me and to others too. But why?'

I have to ask. Doggo has made me suspicious of people who help.

'I owe you one,' says she. 'That cat had me lined up for tea, me for tea, you could say. Now she's all of a heap trying to work out what you're doing. She's forgotten all about me.'

I look over at the cat. It is true. The cat is standing up, her head on one side. She is looking as puzzled as a cat can look.

'Don't mind her,' says Mouse. 'Look,' she says, returning to the problem of the bolt, 'I can get down there, you watch.' She slides down the bolt and squeezes herself alongside it, flat as a leaf. 'And now,' she says, 'I'll push here while you shove at the top. We'll do it, you'll see.'

She's got it all worked out.

'Thank you Mouse,' is all I can say.

'What's going on there?' says Cow. She can hear our voices.

'All's set,' I say, 'now!'

So Woolly heaves (I know he does though I can't see him), and Cow hoists the door up with her shoulder (I know she does though I can't see her either) and I heave sideways until my eyes pop. Mouse pushes with her four tiny feet. I can hear her high breath coming in little whistles.

We rest a moment. And then again.

'Now!' I cry. All together we lift and pull, and push and heave until there is a jolt, a rustle, and the third bolt slides free.

Down falls the bolt, down its groove – and me with it.

'Ooooooh!' I say.

'Whoooooooops,' says Mouse.

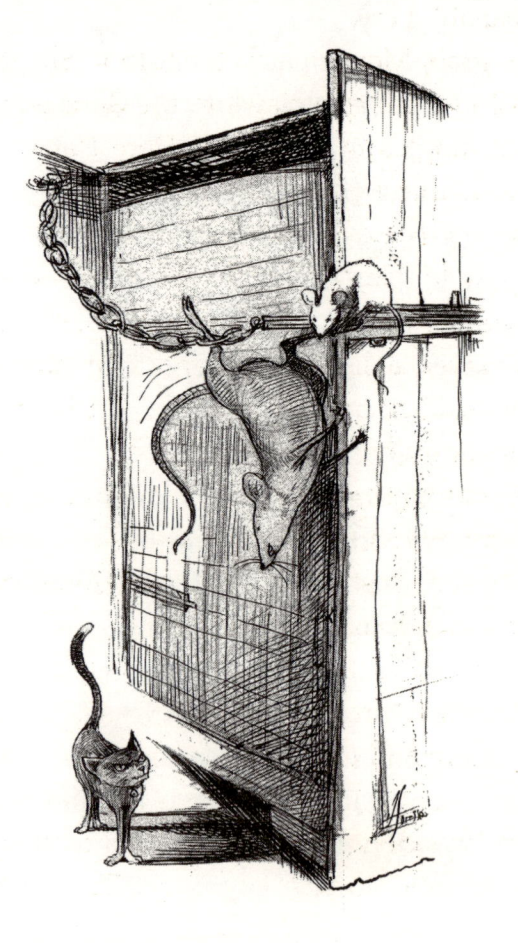

The door swings open, and out. It blows wide in the breeze. It is hanging by a single chain from that toggle in the middle. Mouse and I are hanging onto the door edge for dear life and wishing we had wings.

'Ratty! Ratty! Are you all right?' calls Cow from inside the truck. 'Oh Ratty, what is happening out there?'

Then my claws slip, my feet slide and off I go, out into the air.

'Aaaaaaaah!' I cry.

Snatch, grab, Mouse catches my foot. She gives a pull and I just get two claws to the door edge. My other foot tangles in the chain. Here I am, upside down and helpless as a bat baby.

'Ooooomp!' I say, spinning and breathless. I try to get my paw to something, anything, that will help me turn round and stay on. But no I cannot do it.

Mouse gives a little twist and hop and jump. There she is, back on the top of the truck. She is so small and nimble it is nothing to her this kind of jumping about. But a rat is not made for this either I can tell you. Not a strong-man, and not a gymnast you can be sure. Just a round solid rat thing, and not to be that much longer I fear.

'Oh Ratty!' says Mouse, peering down at me. I can see her face through my back legs. 'You do not look safe there and please, perhaps, if you can, turn your head?'

So I do, upside down though I be. I manage to twist round and look behind me. There, on the ground just a short way off, is the Black Cat.

'You will be squatilated,' says the Black Cat. 'When that ramp comes down, you will be under it. You will be squashed as flat as you can be. A brown rat mat is what you will be some seconds from now.'

I do not need to hear this as you can imagine. Then I hear Cow talking to Woolly.

'I will give a big kick here, Woolly. You go at it with your hard little head and that toggle will burst. I am sure it will. Then Ratty will be safe on the ground and we will be out of here.'

'Oh no Cow...!' I begin to shout but my left claw slips a tadge and I do not finish because I have other things on my mind, like surviving the next half second.

But as I get my claws back into place I think that Black Cat is right. A Rat Mat will be my end unless I think of something.

Cat licks her lips. I think that perhaps she will eat up the Rat Mat and that is another nasty thought. Then I think of something more helpful. It's worth a try, I say to myself.

'*Under the fur,*' I call out, faintly, because my breathing is upside down too. I can't remember much of it, something about hoofs and paws. But that bit I do remember even when I'm upside down. '*Under the fur, friends are we!*'

'Oh goodness me,' says Cat. Her whiskers stiffen

and her ears twitch forward. 'Goodness me. A doggo rhyme. From a rat. Whatever next?' But she has stood up and is peering at me hard.

'Friends under the fur,' I gasp out one last time. She pauses, gives it a moment's thought and then takes a smart step forward.

'A squashed friend is no friend at all,' says she, 'and I would like to know more, like how you know doggo rhymes and why you think a doggo rhyme will stop a cat. You are a brave rat you know to try it, but perhaps you have no choice.'

'Here,' she says, 'when that door falls down, you must jump this way. I will catch you – before I eat you.' She laughs. She is joking, I hope, but what choice do I have I ask you?

'You will have to jump,' she says. 'Push hard with those feet if you can. Aim this way. I am a softer landing than this hard ground you know. I will catch you, I will. Soft paw,' she says, 'promise.'

No more talking time. There is a thunder of hoofs from the van and a splitting noise. Woolly and Cow crash against the swaying door. The toggle snaps and flies into the air. The door drops open with a great clang.

I leap, I push, out into the air. I hover for a moment, but then I'm down, falling down, while the ramp hits the earth with a smacking thump. I spin, I fall and I am scooped out of my dive by two black glossy paws. Above my head I see a bright pink mouth, set about with sharp and pearly teeth.

'Oh mother,' I cry, 'this is it!' I shut my eyes and cat fur folds all round me.

But miracle of miracles, no tooth cuts my skin, no claw slices my fur. I am caught and tossed and caught again. I am a big rat you know and she is not a heavy cat so when I hit into her I knock her over. She is ready for it. She rolls backwards and we bowl over and over across the ground like a two-colour ball until – stop! Stillness! The fur ball uncurls and I slide down, onto my own four feet, safe and sound.

There is a loud noise all about me, and it is not just the beating of my heart and the ringing in my ears. It is people, all about us, people clapping and calling out.

'Hurrah!' they shout. 'An acrobat cat! A circus rat!'

Other people are running up too. There is screaming over by the truck. Someone is frightened I suppose because the door came down with such a crash and Cow and Woolly burst out so fierce and quick. It is chaos, but I am in my fur and breathing, so I am happy as can be.

'Cat,' I say, 'my life is yours. I can never thank you as you deserve.'

'Well friend, still in your fur as you are,' says Cat. 'I did have a certain reputation in my youth for acrobatics but that beat all. I am quite pleased myself. I would like to hear your story but not now perhaps. Where are you living?' She is almost back to her old self already. She is removing the last traces of dust from her back as we speak.

'We are going to a farm in the city. I know that much,' I say, 'but no more than that.'

'Oh the farm is not far,' says she, 'just up the road in fact. I will visit you there... but you will have to go quick or someone will stop you I fear. And your friends need you.'

Right she is. Cow and Woolly are standing dazed at the bottom of the ramp. A crowd is standing round them. The people have stopped screaming because it is difficult to be frightened of Cow and Woolly once you see them as they are.

Then one person starts all over again, because of Mouse, who is peering down from the van roof. But Mouse decides Black Cat is too close and scurries off and the screaming stops again and there is one less noise to deal with.

But then I hear a high bark from the pub, and the sound of a door crashing open. 'Doggo!' I hiss. Black Cat turns her head and takes a step away.

'Cow, Woolly!' I yell. Cow trots over and lowers her head for me.

'Oh Ratty, Ratty dear,' she says, 'you are alive and well. How glad I am.'

Woolly is behind her. 'Ratty,' he says, 'we three are together and that's the way we'll stay, so let us go before our grey foe returns.' He is a fierce lamb and getting fiercer by the hour.

Up I leap onto Cow's head. I scan left and right and see where we can get out of the yard and into the streets beyond.

'This way,' I cry. Cow lifts her big feet and begins to trot. Woolly gallops along beside us waving his head.

'Doggo is coming!' I cry. I see in the corner of my eye a grey streak pushing its way through the press of legs towards us. So off we go at a helter skelter pace into the crowded roads of the city.

'That way, straight ahead,' calls a high miaowing voice. Black Cat, back on the fence now, points her elegant tail to a road straight ahead of us. 'That's the way for you and double quick too.'

So that is the way we go, Cow trotting as fast as a cow can trot and Woolly following on behind. There are even more people here. Getting along is not so easy.

'Animals!' the people cry. 'Animals in the city! Watch out that car there! Let them pass!'

The people are for us, I see. They are not Farmer. They wish us well.

'Let them through,' they call. The cars stop and pull aside. The big red buses come to a halt. All the people inside press their faces to the glass windows and wave and laugh and cheer us. Soon we have a clear path up the middle of the road and no one in our way at all, while all the people cheer and wave and call out to us.

But then, there is a snap and a wuff and a scrabble of paws. There in front of us blocking our way, big and angry and full of himself as ever, is Wall-Eyed Doggo, Farmer's Friend indeed, blocking our way.

'I remember this,' says Doggo. 'We have been here before. I know what happens next.'

'But Doggo,' I say, 'we are not on your farm now. Look about you.' He turns his head and sees the people lining the street and crowding up behind us. 'Do you think, Doggo,' I say, 'that they are on your side?'

He pauses, and he thinks. The people crowd closer. They push about us.

'Let me stroke the cow,' says one.

'What a fine sheep,' says another.

'They are going to the farm,' says a third, 'let us go too.'

Doggo has thought long enough. 'You are right,' says Doggo. 'Wrong place, wrong time.'

He looks around again. A worried look comes in his eye. He stops growling and closes his mouth down over his white teeth. 'Where is Farmer?' he says. 'Where is Farmer when I want him? I need a friend now. Where is Farmer the Doggo's Friend I want to know?'

But Farmer is nowhere. Or rather he is stuck, because I can see his stick waving over the crowd half a mile behind us. He is stuck in this herd of people, red-faced and cross as he can be, and stuck as a fly in honey.

'He will not help you now,' I say. 'Why not help us?'

It does not take him long to decide. Doggos love to be loved as he has said. And Doggo sees about him faces smiling at Cow and Woolly and even me. But they frown at him. Some of them wag their fingers at him.

'Bad Doggo,' says one, 'do not growl at these brave animals.'

He cannot bear it. He must be loved. So there in front of us, he changes. Quick, flash, here's the new Doggo, our Doggo friend, our pal.

'I will come with you,' he says. 'Perhaps I can help clear a way.'

And off he goes ahead of us, not chasing us but running on ahead to clear our path, a humble friend to cow and sheep. Oh if Farmer could see him now, what would he say? 'Never trust a doggo,' that's what he would say. And that's what I say too, unless you know which side that doggo's bone is buttered.

So here we are trotting up that long road, our ears flapping, our eyes dazzled, until the crowd parts and there we see a sharp turn through a gateway to our right and over it in tall red letters – 'The City Farm'.

CHAPTER 10

We should have known. Not plain sailing. Never is.

In we go, and Cow is waving her tail so happily that I feel the breeze of it up by her head. Woolly is dancing as if he had springs in his feet and when he sees another sheep, and then another and then three more, he bleats as though his curly heart will break with joy. Tears come into his steely eyes.

'Heart's joy,' he says. 'A happy place with other sheep, a farm. Here's Somewhere at last!' He dances some more and bleats so loud that the sheep all lift their heads and smile and nod and bleat back to him.

But straight in front of us is a man in a hat. He looks at us and looks at the crowd which stretches back behind us as far as I can see. He tilts his hat back on his head. He puts his hands upon his hips and stands there in our way, like Doggo really. More frightening than Doggo. He guards the way to where we want to be and we don't like that frown upon his face.

'What's all this?' he says. He speaks Animal better than anyone I've ever met. No need for Cinnamon's translating here and a good thing too for he is far away. 'What is all this? Glad to meet you friends, but where are you from? Why are you here? Who are you indeed? And who paid money for you?'

Cruel questions where we hoped for an open door and a full manger.

'No one pays money for a rat,' I say. We are proud, we ratties, we brown wild ratty tribes. We may be hunted high and low. We may be welcome nowhere. But no one buys us. I stand tall on Cow's head and lift my long brown head and stare into Hat Man's puzzled eyes.

'Ah ratty friend,' he says, 'we have a few of your tribe here and we certainly don't pay money for them either. So you are right in that. But you, dear Cow,' he says, 'and you, friend Woolly, someone has paid money for you. That someone will come to us and say we stole you if I take you in.'

He is undecided. He rocks upon his feet and looks behind us at the crowd. How can he say No, now? He is trying to work it out and getting nowhere, when Farmer bursts through the wall of people and shouts as only Farmer can.

'They're mine!' he bellows, 'and they are for the meat factory. Today!'

Well at that, what a noise begins. The people look at each other and mutter, and pass the word back, and mutter more. They look at Farmer as if they think he would be a good parcel for the meat factory. Then they begin to roar.

Never have I heard such a noise and I am a well-travelled ratty as you know. It is like a wind, or more like thunder perhaps, or most like friend Bull when he sees his cows for the first time each year.

The roar starts in the front and moves back, down along the street. Then it comes back, loud, louder, until it breaks at our feet. The people shout and wave their hands and hurl hard words at Farmer. Farmer has never heard the like. His crinkled face is white under its sun-brown skin. His eyes pop. He stands and shakes, a sight I never thought to see.

The man in the hat is dumbstruck too. Or almost.

'Well I never,' he says. 'Whatever next! It seems to me friends that you are here to stay. And I do think,' he says, 'that if these people want you here, they may come and see you here, and that will be good for us too. I have a farm to run,' he says, 'and business is business.'

'So it is!' says Farmer, looking more cheerful than he has looked for a while now. He nods his head to the man in the hat. 'You are not so stupid as you look,' he says. A sweet talker is Farmer.

So the two of them step aside. They bend their heads together while Cow and Woolly and I gaze about us and hope for the best.

Farmer does not need to be loved like Doggo, but he needs to be paid. That is what he seems to be saying to the man in the hat.

'These people do not understand,' he says. 'I have a living to make like any other person here. Animals eat as you know well,' he says, 'and I need money for them. A businessman like you will understand.'

Somehow they reach a bargain. Farmer shakes the Hat Man's hand. Cow lets her breath run loose out of her lungs. She hopes to live now, and Woolly too. It does seem to me that Woolly has been thinking of running off again, perhaps with a woolly friend or two, but now he settles back onto his sharp hoofs and winks his blue eye towards the sheep field, and bends to eat a sprig of grass.

'Home,' he says between his grassy breaths. 'Home.'

But there is still Doggo. He is standing so still that you could miss that he is there. He hopes so. He hopes that Farmer does not see him or that Farmer does not guess that he has helped us. But Farmer is not blind and

Farmer is not stupid. He nods his head across to Doggo where he stands so still.

'Oh Doggo,' says Farmer. 'Doggo, Wall-Eyed Doggo, oldest friend. You are not stupid. You know which side is up. You are not the simple doggo pal I thought you. But so what?' says Farmer. 'Perhaps we make a good team you and I. Let us get back and think again.'

Doggo gets bigger, yes he does. He fluffs up and stands tall and laughs his doggo laugh and flops his long pink tongue out between his ivory white fangs. His cold and marbled eyes shine with joy. Doggos need to be loved and that is that. So Farmer and Farmer's Friend turn to the gate and push through the crowd and the people let them go. Some of them even slap Farmer upon the back.

'Well done,' says one.

'Good work,' says another.

Cameras click and lights flash. Soon I see that someone has grabbed hold of Farmer down the road and is talking to him. There is a man with a big box on his shoulder. 'That is a camera for the telly,' says Hat Man. 'Your Farmer will be on the television tonight, and you too I think if we wait a minute or two.'

Fame! It's a fine thing I'm sure. Though not as good as a full food pail and a shed with a good roof. Not that I expect a food pail, that would be a lot for a ratty but then I don't need one. At this farm there is ratty food on every side and friendly animals willing to share.

The three of us give interviews (we do!). Hat Man translates, as if only people watch those bright square screens in houses. We know Cinnamon will see us, and Black Cat too I think, and even Mouse perhaps. They can tell their human friends the bits that Hat Man doesn't get quite right.

At last the people go, the gates are clanged shut, and all of us creatures are shown to our shelters. We travellers are fed, and the night falls over us. There is no sniffing now, no Doggo hunter on our trail, for we are home at last.

CHAPTER 11

'Well,' says Cinnamon, 'you have landed on your four paws and your eight hoofs here, I must say.'

He finishes off the creamy milk that our new friend Lisette from Jersey has given him. 'I've not had milk like that since I was a kitten with my eyes tight shut,' says he.

Lisette smiles and nods her long horns. She is justly proud. She has a rosette on the fence of her pen that says she is the creamiest cow this side of town and she likes to be appreciated.

Cow, my Cow, our Cow, is leaning against the gatepost, scratching her long black and white neck and humming to herself. Milking is not her thing, never will be, wrong temperament all along as I could have told you, probably did. But nobody minds that here. You know her. You can imagine.

Everyone here loves Cow and so do the people who come to visit.

'Where is the cow I saw in the street?' they ask.

They have their photo taken standing next to her while she waves her tail and looks modest. If they can find him they try to get Woolly Woolly Baa Lamb in the picture but he is hard to find because he is with his sheep friends, telling them what's what. He is a fierce and bold lambkin. There is no doubt about that. He is a hero from another world to the gentle lambs here and they follow him everywhere.

Today Cinnamon has come to see us. He has brought Tall Lady and Roly Man with him. They are in the office talking to our other friends, the people who look after us.

'All's well that ends well,' they say.

On the fence is sitting Black Cat. She calls in most days to see us. She saved my life and so for me she is the Cat of Cats. Perhaps she thinks that Cinnamon is Cat of Cats for her. She has not seen him before and she is gazing with astonishment at his pale and sultry fur. He half closes his blue crystal eyes and pretends not to notice.

Mouse has moved in completely, with her whole family. 'Show a mouse a good thing,' she says, 'and there we'll be, families and all. Good company here,' says she, 'and even these cats – what a pleasure to meet cats who can keep their claws to themselves.'

It is strange. I have laughed at doggos who must be loved but perhaps we all like it if we have the chance. Here the children come and feed us and stroke us. Hat Man is our friend, and all the visitors smile and joke with us and wish us happy. It is like living in sunshine.

All I will say is that we ratties do like a bit of excitement. We like a thrill or two. It keeps us dancing on our ratty paws. So I lie here in the hay, contented as can be, warm, full, and smiling. But my beady eyes are on the lookout. So, where is the next adventure? That is what I say.

Everyone here loves Cow and so do the people who come to visit.

'Where is the cow I saw in the street?' they ask.

They have their photo taken standing next to her while she waves her tail and looks modest. If they can find him they try to get Woolly Woolly Baa Lamb in the picture but he is hard to find because he is with his sheep friends, telling them what's what. He is a fierce and bold lambkin. There is no doubt about that. He is a hero from another world to the gentle lambs here and they follow him everywhere.

Today Cinnamon has come to see us. He has brought Tall Lady and Roly Man with him. They are in the office talking to our other friends, the people who look after us.

'All's well that ends well,' they say.

On the fence is sitting Black Cat. She calls in most days to see us. She saved my life and so for me she is the Cat of Cats. Perhaps she thinks that Cinnamon is Cat of Cats for her. She has not seen him before and she is gazing with astonishment at his pale and sultry fur. He half closes his blue crystal eyes and pretends not to notice.

Mouse has moved in completely, with her whole family. 'Show a mouse a good thing,' she says, 'and there we'll be, families and all. Good company here,' says she, 'and even these cats – what a pleasure to meet cats who can keep their claws to themselves.'

It is strange. I have laughed at doggos who must be loved but perhaps we all like it if we have the chance. Here the children come and feed us and stroke us. Hat Man is our friend, and all the visitors smile and joke with us and wish us happy. It is like living in sunshine.

All I will say is that we ratties do like a bit of excitement. We like a thrill or two. It keeps us dancing on our ratty paws. So I lie here in the hay, contented as can be, warm, full, and smiling. But my beady eyes are on the lookout. So, where is the next adventure? That is what I say.